A

COLLECTION

OF

DARK SHORT

STORIES

The Short Stories Collections

Also, by Sean Haughton

The George & Sally Series

Guided by the Ghosts

The Secret in The Breeze*

The Summer of '16

The Tragedy of the Ghosts (Short Story Prequel)

Poetry

Reflections: Fifty Poems*

Second Wave

The Short Stories Collections

A Collection of Dark Short Stories

*Also available in Audiobook format

A

COLLECTION

OF

DARK SHORT

STORIES

The Short Stories Collections

SEAN HAUGHTON

For the little one, gone

ACKNOWLEDGEMENTS

With loving thanks, as ever, to my family.

Gratitude must also be shown to Ash Watson & Lo Potter for their constant shows of support & encouragement. Keep on shining.

Thanks also to Liz & Laurelle for their support, humour & for constantly keeping me occupied.

Contents

My Death Is In My Dream

I feel the world fall into view.

Unnatural, glazed, with my arms tinted with the numbness you usually feel when you've lay on them in bed. Blurred sounds take an eternity to clear, but clear they eventually do, and I hear music drifting from the phonograph. Delicate piano and slow saxophones paint the air with atmosphere, and I find myself stood in the centre of my living room. I am fully clothed and booted, with my trench coat buttoned and my fedora in my hand ready to be placed onto my head. I remember a time when I would feel a kiss on my cheek at this point, with a sweet voice setting me up for the day.

"Have a good day at work, Arthur, dear."

But she's not here anymore. Now, there is only the music for company, the only thing that breaks the silence inside these walls. I make my way towards the front door, putting on the fedora as I step out. The phonograph is left on, and yet, despite me leaving the house, the music doesn't subside, it stays with me. The outside air is cold, the surroundings are other worldly. I begin my usual walk, which will eventually lead me to the train station, where I will board my transport to work. As I walk, there is a peculiar aura, the essence that makes the usual sight of my street seem like something I have never known, nor seen before. The houses are the same, and the occasional faces I see are the same, and yet... it is all so alien to me.

As though something is being hidden, as though these houses are placards ready to fall and reveal a stage, and the faces are masks ready to reveal actors & actresses who are playing a part in some great manipulation. Still the music plays, but that is the only sound I can hear. Were it not for the music, there would be complete silence; not even my footsteps can be heard, regardless of how heavy my feet hit the floor, step by step.

My hands are in my pockets, yet I can barely feel them. I barely feel alive, physically. As I walk, I ponder what has brought me to this position. I make my morning trip to work every day, the same monotonous routine that sees me walk from home to the station, catch the train to work, walk to work, and then fulfil that routine in reverse come the evening. Since my love passed, life has lost meaning. Many times, I have considered checking out of life, altogether, but such thoughts usually subside immediately once I am reminded how entry to Heaven is forbidden to those who end their time on Earth with premature intent, and indeed if Heaven exists, then I know my beloved will be there, and I wish to see her again. If suffering through this meaningless life allows me to discover her once all this is said and done, then so be it.

I find myself trying to find joy in the little things, like the conversations you hear people having around you, or the ageing faces you see, year on year. Trying to find joy in the way the world around us evolves, wondering what the future holds. In reminding myself of this desire, I remember how those conversations are absent while I walk, as again I can still only hear the music. How is this possible? The distance between myself and the phonograph back home grows with every passing step, and yet I may as well be sat back in my chair in the living room, with the sounds consuming my mind as they enter my ears. Still, the pleasant tones make for an enjoyable listen, a delicate continuation of various gentle Jazz themes. Vocals not necessary, the music is all that's required.

Continuing my walk, I see a signpost directing me to the station. I see this same signpost every day, and yet today, there is a man underneath it. He is watching me as I walk, occasionally glancing around, as though he is mindful of being watched, himself. He, too, is wearing a trench coat and fedora, with his collar guarding his cheeks. The clothes are a greyish-black tone, and he wears a thick moustache. But his eyes... his eyes are cold, and cruel. He is a man seemingly of intent, and he watches me further as I walk past him, my eyes discretely following him as I do. I have never seen this man before in my life, let alone under this sign. As I carry on, I glance behind me. The man isn't following me, not yet anyway, but he has turned ever so slightly to keep track of my movements. I feel a hint of fear begin to seep into my psyche, but I am mindful of the need to be at the train station with enough time to spare, and so I carry on as normal, hoping the man is of no connection to me and that I can get on with my day. Eventually, I reach the station, and at last a secondary sound joins the music, as the slightest tones of hustle & bustle can be heard. I take a copy of the usual morning newspaper, but peculiarly the man I regularly buy the paper from has a blank expression on his face. Still, my surroundings feel as alien as earlier, even though I know them so well. The paper seller moves his lips, but no sound escapes from his mouth. Whether it is drowned out by the music & the noise of the station, I cannot be sure. I try to figure out what he is saying, but to no avail. I walk away, paper in hand, without actually paying for it, but this doesn't seem so strange. I make my way towards my usual platform, sitting down on my usual bench. I have around ten minutes to spare, allowing me to digest the news before I catch the train to work.

And there is nothing. The paper carries only the usual logo at the top of the front page, but there is no headline, no pictures, not even a date. I flick through the paper and see blank templates where pictures and text should adorn each page. Even the sport is blank, the Division One table that should be reflecting the football season's progress instead looking like a blank box, as though the clubs have all been declared defunct. The fine detail in the world is in a state of flux; it seems so present and yet has simultaneously vanished. I look up from the paper, I can feel the bemusement and confusion in my face. A mist has gathered inside the station, and I have to strain my eyes to see the trains as they arrive and depart. I glance around, but there is nobody around me. Nobody. I look forward, and see the man again. The man from before, with the moustache and the cold, cruel eyes. He is partially stood behind one of the large, tall pillars that hold the station aloft, and he stares not simply at me, but into my soul. And he stares with an almost delicate hatred. I cautiously share his stare, with my head turned ever so slightly. I try to remain calm and collected, but I can feel the fear building within me, but fear of what, I do not know. Maybe it is the knowledge that I am alone in this age-old train station with this mysterious man, with a mysterious mist gathering around us. I try to challenge my mind, to see if I know where this man is from, but every time I think the metaphorical finger in my mind lingers over the button, the button seems to move. I find myself suddenly at the edge of the platform, ready to board my usual train, which slowly begins to arrive. The music from the phonograph finally evaporates, the sounds replaced by the noise emanating from the train. Usually, I am surrounded by my fellow commuters, but alas, the station remains empty, aside from myself and the moustache man, who has conveniently disappeared. At least, I think he has, until I suddenly feel a great force into my back that leaves me falling in front of the oncoming train, as everything descends into darkness.

Part Two: The Reality

I feel the world fall into view.

Sounds signal the start of a new day, as the real world comes into being as I awaken, though my right arm is tinted with the numbness that typically comes as I've lay on it in bed. I take a number of deep breaths to allow myself the ability to make sense of my surroundings, and in the distance, delicate piano and slow saxophones paint the air with atmosphere, and I smile knowing the phonograph will be playing in the living room. I raise myself from my bed, wishing I could allow its comfort to consume me for the day, but alas, another normal day awaits. I rub my face, ridding my senses of the dreariness that naturally comes with the end of a night's sleep, and in doing so, last night's dream colonizes my thoughts. The music on the phonograph, the bizarre walk to work, the silent seller, the mist in the train station, the moustache man... and a world without my beloved. Suddenly, I feel a cold chill rush through me, and I can only sit in silence, fearful of the idea of such a nightmarish world. But then, the silence is broken.

"Breakfast is ready, darling."

There she is. My beloved Rita. A new calm washes away the doom, like a bucket of boiling water representing reality being poured over a frozen puddle representing the darkness in my dream. I rise, stretching out the cracks in my joints across my body, and slowly stroll out of my bedroom and down the stairs into the hallway. My fedora and trench coat hang on the coat stand, ready for the usual trip to work which will begin sooner than I'm ready for, but no matter, breakfast and a brief spell with my sweetheart will give me all the energy I need. As I enter the living room, she is there at the table, her beautiful head swaying to the music.

"Morning, Arthur, dear," her sweet lips say, as I wander over to her for the embrace that I cherish the most. The darkness that clouded my dream does not exist in the real world. I am reminded of the mist that soaked the air in the train station, in contrast with how my beloved's natural beam fills the living room.

"Ready for another day, sweetheart?" she asks. I ponder for a moment, my body language perhaps revealing how much I'd rather stay here.

"I suppose so," I answer. "Hopefully it passes by quickly enough and I can get back to where I belong; in front of the fire with you and the music."

Rita chuckles; her smile alone will give me strength to last the entire day. Nonetheless, there remains a lingering darkness in the back of my mind. Maybe it is the aftermath of my dream. It is not so uncommon to be hindered by a dream after it has taken place, but I do my best to focus on the real as opposed to the imaginary. What is real in this world is where I am right now, not lost in some demonic interpretation of the train station. It is not long however before I realise I must set off for my usual trip, and so I rise from the table to go and clean and dress myself, before returning downstairs, where I collect the fedora and trench coat from the coat stand. As I put them on,

Rita stands in the living room doorway, but she looks somewhat sombre. I try to share with her the warmth she has gifted to me.

"Be well without me, my dearest," I say to her. "Don't have too much fun until I return."

"Just make sure you DO return, Arthur. I don't want to live a life in which you're not there anymore."

Her words, usually so warming, are now troubling to me. I can only smile weakly as a means of trying to reassure her.

"Worry not, my love. I will always be there."

With those words said, we share a kiss, and before I leave, I cherish the sight of her. Yet still, she looks scared, as though her own dreams were filled with quiet horror.

"Goodbye, Arthur, my love."

"Until later, lovely Rita."

And with that, I leave the house, beginning my stroll to the train station. I feel the need to test myself and my surroundings, just to make sure that the darkness in the dream can be pushed away. It is cold, and my hands are in my pockets, but I can feel them, something only recognized as I grip the insides of the pockets, almost to make a point to myself. There is sound, but it is not the music escaping from the phonograph at home, instead it is the collective noise birthed by the coming together of passing vehicles, the chatter of locals and, probably my favourite of the lot, the sound of my boots.

"Morning Arthur!"

It is the gentleman from over the road, John, wearing his trusty blue & white scarf as he too prepares to head to work.

"Morning John! How's the family?" I cheerfully reply.

His big old grin beams across his face, as he says "Just grand, my friend! Have a fine day!"

And so, I carry on strolling, a jovial spring in my step that wasn't present in my dream. The world around me, often so grey as it was last night, seems to be bathing in joy. I am almost alarmed by the contrast, but this alarm quickly subsides as I see people smiling and laughing in the face of the harsh nature of the cold. Eventually, I reach the signpost in which the moustache man appeared last night. A hint of ice runs through my veins at the thought of his appearance, and I almost feel the aggressive push in my back that left me underneath the oncoming train...

But of course, the moustache man isn't there, because he doesn't exist. He was nothing more than a disturbing creation of the darkest corners of my mind, possibly formed through a collaboration of my worst fears. Maybe dreams have multiple purposes. Maybe the best dreams are there to inspire us, to reveal to us what we wish to achieve, or what we could achieve with effort, whereas our nightmares allow us to witness what we truly fear, or perhaps represent a phantom hybrid of unspeakable fears that we cannot properly identify.

Either way, if last night achieved anything, it stimulated my mind and enforced me with a sense of appreciation for the world I wander through each day. Maybe, just maybe, there is something good about the world outside my front door.

I enter the train station, and make my way towards the paper stand. Peculiarly, in the dream, I just collected a copy, and the paper seller just stood there, almost ghost-like, almost possessed. Today, of course, he is there, swapping paper for coin and wishing the commuters a good day and to enjoy their read. He recognizes me as I walk towards him.

"Ah, one of my regulars, how are you today, good sir?" he booms.

"You know what, my friend," I reply, "I think today might just be one to remember for a long time. I've got an awfully good feeling!"

"That's the spirit, my good man! That'll be a Penny, as usual!"

I take my paper, and bid the man farewell until tomorrow. Once again, such a contrast to last night.

I make my way towards my usual platform, sitting down on my usual bench. I have around ten minutes to spare, allowing me to digest the news before I catch the train to work. And this time, the paper has plenty of detail; the day's news, the latest stories, the Division One table... I have to suppress a little chuckle, as I find myself utterly amused by the contrast of the fear in my dream and my delight at such minute details of this, the latest in a series of normal days.

But then, something happens. Something that runs my blood cold. Painfully cold, like when the frost chews your hands raw on a bitter winter's night.

I look up from my paper, and I look towards the pillar, and see him. The man who doesn't exist.

The moustache man.

Impossible... he doesn't exist!

But something else takes me aback. In my dream, he was a figure of darkness, his cold and cruel eyes piercing my soul as he eyed me with hateful intent.

But this moustache man, standing in front of the pillar rather than leering behind it, reading his own copy of today's paper, doesn't appear cold or cruel at all.

On the contrary, he appears almost... weak, and timid. There is nothing particularly intimidating about him, but last night he took my life.

No. In my dream, he took my life. Maybe I have seen him during my usual morning commute and never paid much attention, but my mind turned him into a nightmare.

As I ponder such lunacy, he has turned his head to look at me. He notices the horror in my face, and his own face is full of confusion. He is taken aback. He doesn't know me, nor does he recognize me, but he knows that I am horrified by his presence. But then something else happens...

The moustache man glances ever so slightly to my right, and now HE is in shock. Now HE is horrified. But why?

That's when it happens. Something explodes into my stomach, and I struggle to comprehend existence itself. I quickly begin to feel numb, almost non-existent, and I look to my right, to where the moustache man had looked before he appeared so horrified. And that's when I see him, a man with an empty face. My real murderer, who simply sits there having shot his gun. My hands tremble as I move them over my wound, where blood haemorrhages from within me, like my soul escaping my physical form. It is in this moment that I realise that my death was not in my dream, but was instead in my reality.

It is also then that I realise that this is the end of my story.

Detective

"We're really gonna need you on this one. Just go from scene to scene, take as long as you need. Try and support your understudies the best you can, they'll need your experience on this, in every way."

These were the tired words of the Superintendent near the end of his call roughly an hour ago. I was awoken by the phone ringing, and when I answered I received his immediate apologies, which quickly progressed into him requesting that I come into work on my day off. Well, not exactly come into work as such, more make my way to what was apparently a particularly gruesome crime scene, then head off to another, and then another. Three different crime scenes, all with units based at each of them, and all with near-traumatised groups of officers trying to make sense of the apparent horror that awaits me.

There's one common theme, though: there are no bodies to be found.

I assured the Superintendent that he could count on me, and I dragged myself out of bed as I readied myself for what was to come.

Eventually, I leave my house behind and enter the outside world, where a damp drizzle awaits me, accompanied by a relatively dour feel to the air, before I begin the drive to the first crime scene where, as I get out of my car outside the home of the first victim, I am welcomed by a familiar young PC who looks particularly affected by what she has seen.

PC Mercer is approaching 30, and has been with the force for about four years now. She's always had a good head on her, eager to do right by people and often hellbent on putting criminals behind bars. She's impressed me whenever I've seen her in action; gentle with victims when necessary, firm with suspects at just the right moments and brutal with wrongdoers when it's absolutely deserved.

But today, she wears a face I've not seen before. Maybe her strong, previous fronts have been masks, and today I'm seeing her true self for the first time as she encounters the apparent horrors I was informed of by the Superintendent.

Maybe today I meet the real PC Mercer for the very first time...

"Morning, Chief Inspector," she says with a delicate whimper, despite her admirable efforts to put on a show of bravery.

I calmly reply "Morning, PC Mercer. Fancy talking me through what we've got on our hands."

She gulps, and pauses for a split second. She has exposed her own fears immediately, clearly not wishing to head back inside, but to her credit she remains professional, and as we walk side-by-side towards the front door, she begins to provide a breakdown of what is known about this particular scene.

"I can't say I've ever seen anything like this before, Chief," she says, a nervous chill running through her teeth. "You know better than anyone how much pride I put into this job, but it's days like this you dread. The kind of day you hope never comes, and when it does, you're not entirely sure how to react, or whether you're truly cut out for all this."

I pause just before we head inside, and make a point of turning to face her.

"Mercer, you're a damn good officer, but do me a favour and toughen up!" I say quietly but coldly. "Days like today are what make us. It's the days like today that we must face down, because when we do, then we're ready to face anything. And that's exactly how it's supposed to be."

Mercer audibly gulps, though her efforts to keep it quiet clearly leave a sudden pain in her throat.

"Sorry, Chief," she mumbles. "I just wasn't ready for today."

"No one ever is at first," I reply. "But you will be in future."

Together, myself and PC Mercer step inside and immediately her knees nearly buckle, though to her credit she makes a quick recovery. There is blood on the hallway walls, albeit in smatters, but I can tell this is merely a teaser for what is to come. I carry on into the living room, where I am welcomed by a most heinous scene.

It's red. Everywhere is red. I'd say the walls have been given a fresh coat, but I'm absolutely certain B&Q don't stock blood red.

The smell is... well, I'd rather not say. It's hardly surprising that young Mercer was so eager to stay outside. The cold majestic air is something to cherish on even the most uneventful day, but today it must seem like a commodity to these young officers. Even those more experienced heads in their forties and upwards seem shellshocked, which may somewhat impact what I was telling Mercer about days like today toughening one up.

I glance at her, and see she's eager to escape the horror surrounding her, even while the rain falls outside. Lennon once sang that "*when the rain comes, they run and hide their heads, they might as well be dead,*" and yet today I'm surrounded by people who would rather bathe in the rain than remain part of this scene of death.

Ironic.

However, as cruel as it may seem, I instead beckon Mercer to follow me as I stroll around the room. Such is the monstrosity I find myself in that I actually step into a puddle of blood on the carpet. Can you imagine that? We've all spilt something on the carpet at some point or another in our lives, even something as menial as a glass of water, and it's always a bit icky when you trod in it. But this... an actual puddle of blood pushing up from out of the carpet and beginning to add fresh character to the soul of my boots. Mercer notices and nearly throws up. Poor girl. Her talents are potentially limitless, but right now she lacks the stomach to be here too long. She lacks the strength necessary. She'll need to learn, hence why I insist on keeping her here just a little bit longer.

I stand in silence for a moment, glancing around at the scene, before suddenly asking Mercer "Do we know who the house belongs to?"

Quickly straightening herself up, she answers "We believe so, Sir."

I, again, make a point of looking at her.

"Well," I say, somewhat bluntly, "who is it?"

She gulps again. "Alec Smith, Sir."

Silence reigns momentarily, before I break it.

"THE Alec Smith?" I ask, quietly, despite the emphasis on 'the.'

"Yes, sir," Mercer replies. "This is where he moved to after he was released, it would seem." I glance around at the walls once more, and see the blood with different eyes. Alec Smith was a notorious killer, not that it mattered in the eyes of our beloved justice system. The wig wearers in the courts deemed him safe to walk the streets, despite every bit of evidence proving otherwise. Thinking about Smith and his crimes reminds me of what Mercer said outside about being cut out for this job. I'd been in the force for years before the Smith case, so I should've been ready for the brutality, as well as the disappointment of seeing the wigs let yet another scumbag get off easy. And yet still, seeing him serve a pitiful sentence before walking free nearly pushed me over the edge. The families he tore apart had been failed, with countless other families potentially at risk...

Instead, he went quiet. I suppose I should've been grateful, but he had been given a fresh chance when he should've been rotting in a cell. I hardly see it as a consolation that he didn't take another life.

Still, it would seem that he's had what was coming to him a long time ago. Not that I'm supposed to think like that, of course. But the bitterness remains...

I have a little huff and a puff to myself, before meeting Mercer's eyes and giving her a little side-nod to allow her to leave. She gratefully nods and hastily exits the living room, before quickly dashing through the hallway and returning to the outside world. She'll have a great career, that much I'm certain. She'll be cursing me for keeping her in here when she was so desperate to stay outside, but I stand by what I said earlier.

She'll need to learn. And she will.

I take one last glance around at the room, my facial expression one of disgust at the scene of Smith's seemingly bloody end, and then I too begin to make my way out of the living room, through the hallway and back outside through the front door. The rain falls gently, as Mercer awaits my exit from the property.

"So, what now, Sir?" she asks as I kick my heels into the concrete, hoping to rid my boots of some of the blood.

"I straighten up and carry on to the second scene," I reply. "Keep your chin up, Mercer. I meant what I said earlier, you're a damn good officer. Get a couple of strong ones down you after your shift. Remember, days like today are what make you."

She nods, and pushes through a brave grin. Hopefully she'll take some comfort in the knowledge that the victim wasn't exactly innocent. Either way, I get back into my car and begin the drive to the next scene, as the windscreen wipers brushing away the rain remind me of how Smith's blood will need to be cleaned away from his walls.

The vulgar smell hasn't left my nostrils. The smell of Smith's blood plastered over his walls. I roll the car window down slightly to let some fresh air combat the obscenity plaguing my nasal senses, but that battle appears to be a losing one. Instead, I can feel spits of rain coming in & hitting the side of my face as I drive.

It's quite the comical hybrid of pleasant sensation and irritating distraction.

Soon enough, however, I arrive at my destination.

Scene Two.

Again, I am welcomed by a familiar face, one who also looks as though he'd rather be somewhere else. PC Gates is roughly five years older than PC Mercer, but he's a good fella.

Like Mercer, he craves justice, and in tandem with his likeable personality, he's become an asset to the force. Having been leaning on the front garden wall, he straightens himself up and gives his wet hair a ruffle.

"Morning, Sir," he says grimly, albeit with a weak, half-grin.

"Morning, PC Gates," I reply. "You look worse for wear, my friend."

"You're about to find out why, Chief," Gates mutters. "These are the days I really hope to avoid."

"Aye," I puff out, "Mercer was the same at Scene One, but as I reminded her, these are the days you need to take advantage of. Cruel and as brutal as they are, they make you a far better officer for it in the long-term."

"So they say, Sir," Gates replies, not quite convinced. "Shall we step inside?"

I nod. "No time like the present. What do we know about the victim?"

"Well, for starters Sir, I think he was one of your old cases."

I stop in my tracks a couple of feet away from the front door, and turn to face my colleague.

"Come again, Gates?"

"What I said, Sir," he replies. "This house belongs to somebody called Derek Lee. If I'm not mistaken, it's the same fraudster you had to deal with at one point, isn't it?"

Derek Lee.

Quite a different kind of scumbag to Alec Smith. Lee conned countless pensioners out of their life savings. Sickeningly enough, the stress he caused led to the deaths of some of his victims. Arguably even more sickening was, you guessed it, the lenient sentence he was handed by the wigs.

Funny isn't it? How you can con the system or the banks out of millions, if not billions, and be handed a century and a half long sentence if you're caught, but screw the common man and woman out of the fruits of their labour and it's hardly worth mentioning, even when the victims are in their twilight years. You can't imagine the shame I felt being lambasted by some of the family members of the victims, particularly the relatives of victims who'd succumbed to the stress and trauma. Most of the relatives knew full well I'd done all I could, but they needed to let loose their anger and frustration, and I stood and took the brunt. It was the least I could do.

I owed them that much.

"Are you still with me, Sir?"

"Hm? Oh, of course."

I nod towards the door, gesturing with an open palm to emphasise my desire for him to lead the way, which he does so. I follow him inside, and once again the hallway is immediately characterized by menial blood stains. A couple on the walls, some on the carpet. Again, it's merely a teaser for what is to come.

We step into the living room, and instantly I know that my nose will be cursing me for the rest of the day, because it is only going to suffer more after this. Another fresh coat of blood plasters the walls, and yet again, the smell is repugnant. Such a contrast to the smell of fresh paint, which is something that I've always seemed to enjoy.

Gates, like Mercer before him, is desperate to be outside and away from the scene, but to his credit he is standing firm, although he can't help but recoil at the smell and sight. What he wouldn't give to be back outside in the rain, but he has duties to adhere to, that much he knows.

And he too must learn. Learn to be strong, learn to battle on.

Learn to simply *cope*.

After all, if the likes of Mercer and Gates can't *cope*, then how else will the force *cope* when I finally get the chance to enjoy retirement? Heaven forbid I get an apologetic call-and-request from the Superintendent at least once a month after I've finally been able to put my feet on the pouffe!

"What are we thinking, Sir?" Gates asks, a contorted look on his face. "Possibly a relative of one of Lee's fraud victims?"

"Possibly so, my friend," I reply, gazing around the room. "But it doesn't equate to the first scene, and there's another to visit after this. No body to be found, just a living room repainted in the victim's blood. What would connect Smith with Lee?"

Gates takes a moment to ponder.

"Vigilantism, maybe?"

"Possibly," I nod in semi-agreement. "But there's somewhat of a difference between vigilantism and outright murder, especially when it's so... artistic."

For the briefest moment, Gates wears a look of horror, until he composes himself.

"Artistic? I'm not sure I'd call this artistic, Chief..."

"No? I'd say whoever is doing this certainly has quite an adventurous approach."

I see a concerned look grow on Gates' face, and quickly put him at ease.

"Don't worry, my friend, there's no justification for all of this on my part. At times you're almost resigned to an eccentric approach to detective work, it allows one to bat away the obscenity of what lies beneath the surface."

Gates allows himself a sigh as he comes to understand what I'm getting at.

"Again, though, no body," I mumble to myself, absently.

"That stood out to me as well, Chief," Gates says. "It's almost as though the victim was drained and..."

His voice evaporates as he quickly realises what he's about to suggest.

"Go on, Gates," I press him. "Drained and...?"

He swallows a hard lump, shudders and resumes.

"It's almost as though the victim was drained of their blood and then simply... disappeared. I know it sounds ridiculous, but I'm speaking more from a philosophical perspective here."

"I understand," I reply, nodding as I do. "It would seem to me that the killer is using the blood as symbolism, leaving it behind to coat the walls of the victims as a lasting monument not only to the vulgarity of their deaths, but also to the vulgarity of their crimes."

Gates' eyebrows pop up momentarily. "So, you think it *is* vigilantism?"

"I'll repeat what I said moments ago," I reply quietly, "Possibly."

Silence takes over, aside from little splotches of blood bouncing up from the carpet as I walk around the room. So much for me kicking Smith's blood off at the last site! I'll have a biological mutation growing on my boots by the end of the day!

But these boots are bearing the brunt, so I thank them.

Eventually, I nod over to Gates, giving him the green light to get back outside. Like Mercer before him, he gratefully nods and hurries back into the outside world. Before I join him, I pause for a moment, as a voice rings in my ears.

My dear old Mum worked all those years for nothing, and now she's gone! All because some parasite took her to the cleaners, and now he's basically got off scot-free! He doesn't even deserve to live!

Ah, yes. A daughter of one of the victims. Fire burned in her eyes, and I couldn't say a word in response, because she was right!

And I failed her, just like I failed her Mother, and all the other victims and their families.

Just like I failed Smith's victims.

Just like I failed...

"Chief?"

Gates has returned, and his voice brings me back to Earth.

"Yes?"

"It's PC Rawls, Sir. He's waiting for you at the next site, I think he's getting a bit desperate."

An audible sigh escapes me, before I leave the living room behind without looking back. Gates leads the way back outside, and as I follow him, I am welcomed by a steady downpour. It cleanses me momentarily of the darkness that lingered in my solitude a moment ago, and I'm grateful.

I say my goodbyes to Gates and his haunted colleagues, their faces very similar to those I saw earlier with Mercer. No doubt the same kind of faces await me at Scene Three.

I spot a puddle on the ground, a more friendly kind this one, and instead of kicking the blood from my boots, I bathe them in the puddle. In doing so, I am almost left with a hint of guilt, as the blood begins to bastardise the puddle and rob it of its purity.

Quite symbolic, when I think about.

It's much like how days like today bastardise the world we live in and steal purity from the innocent.

***

Scene Three.

Knowing I was coming here was why I was so grateful to be bathed in the rain at Scene Two. A brief baptism to cleanse me of darkness and prepare me as I step on cursed ground.

The home of the third victim; Frederick Levy.

The term 'victim' doesn't really suit him. Let's just go with 'deceased.'

I pause for a moment after I pull up, gazing over at the house with hatred locking my jaw and burning my eyes. It's only when PC Rawls & PC Johnson notice my arrival and begin to encroach into my line of sight do I allow the tension to settle somewhat. Speaking of Rawls & Johnson...

Look at these poor bastards. They look like they've shit themselves. Unlike Mercer & Gates, Rawls & Johnson fall into the mature category of officer. Genuinely good blokes, but they definitely weren't made for days like today. Mercer & Gates will grow and evolve. These two poor buggers will be on the lash for weeks after this.

"M-morning, Chief," Rawls stutters. "Thanks for getting here so quickly."

"Don't mention it," I reply bluntly. "I'm guessing you two are struggling somewhat?"

"Us and everyone else here, Sir," Johnson pipes up. "I'll be on the lash for weeks after this!"

Told you.

"Fine," I sigh lazily. "You pair stay out here; we don't want you spewing up on the crime scene do we. I'll be back shortly."

And so, I leave them behind, their relief rather obvious even as I move further away from them as I make my way towards the front door. If their mild relief can spread from metres away, then clearly the darkness that emanates from this property can spread for miles. I feel it as I step inside, and such is my loathing for this place and the man who called it home, I feel no sorrow nor sympathy as I again see the blood stains on the hallway walls.

Don't ask me to go into details about the crimes of Frederick Levy. I don't think I've ever recovered from that case, nor do I think I ever will. Let's just say he preyed on the young and leave it at that!

I step into the living room, and a million memories overwhelm me at once. Years of cases, from the mere menial to the very worst. Levy was at the top of the ladder. The worst thing I've ever encountered. Yes, *thing*! Not even human!

And yes, before you ask, the wigs let him off easy.

Reflecting on the damage Derek Lee did, though not easy, was certainly bearable. Reflecting on the cruelty & brutality of Alec Smith was harder, but it certainly provided steel.

Reflecting on Frederick Levy has almost always pushed me to the edge of the abyss. No amount of alcohol could ever drive away the destruction he left in his wake. I, of course, always have to remind myself that I wasn't the victim of his atrocities, but it doesn't make it any easier. The damage that case did to me... I don't think anybody should have to experience. A part of me instantly died the day that case was assigned to me, and further parts quickly decayed and disintegrated the longer it went on. Like I said, I've never really recovered.

But why Derek Lee? Why Alec Smith? Why Frederick Levy? And why are their murders so similar? Gates seemed to have his finger on the pulse earlier when he mentioned vigilantism on the part of the killer. This killer, this vigilante, knows what these three men did, and sees that they never truly faced justice, and so decided that it was time that they did.

Very different crimes committed, but each a set of atrocities in their own way. Each that left a permanent mark on those who live with the experience, whether as an officer, detective or relative.

Let's break it down.

Humanity is a collective slave to finance and capital. Money causes nothing but stress and hardship, and we are forever chasing it simply as a means to live. Derek Lee tapped into the fear that money creates and used it to bankroll his existence at the expense of those who had spent decades trying to fight back against that fear to allow themselves to get by. In doing so, his victims suffered grief and trauma to such an extent that some are no longer with us. Those who are will now spend their remaining years suffering not only from the pain of losing the money but having to survive without it. Their relatives will need to bear the burden of supporting the victims even more than would be expected as a result, causing greater stress and fracture to their own lives, while the relatives of the deceased will never be able to see past the lost faces of their loved ones whenever they encounter money.

Death, meanwhile, is inevitable, but to encounter death prior to one's due date at the hands of another without due course or justification is in itself a bastardisation of nature. This is what Alec Smith was committing. Not simply murder, but a bastardisation of nature, and he took great pleasure in doing so. Again, those who are left behind are left to bear the brunt, to wear the chains of grief & mourning, and to have to wake everyday knowing what became of their loved ones, and of the manner in which they lost their lives, to the man who took such maniacal joy from it, and how they were failed by a system that has failed us all in so many different ways.

And then...

Then, there is the most heinous of crimes. When you lay your hands on the young with such vile intent, you lose whatever humanity resided in you. You destroy their innocence, permanently thieving it and crushing it for your own sick desires. You leave them with the scars for life, if they are able to survive. You leave their parents and relatives with the heartbreaking notion that they believe they failed them, that they couldn't protect them. You bastardise nature even worse than when a murder is committed, for you murder your own soul and that of a child in the most despicable way imaginable. That's what Frederick Levy did over and over and over and over again.

And now his blood dons the living room walls of this pit he called home. Now, he resides in hell.

You see, I don't know how much longer I have left on Earth. I'm not sure whether my body will eventually pack up or whether I'll drive myself into oblivion, but those who will follow me, those who possess the responsibility to protect the people, and to ensure justice is maintained, must be ready. They must possess the steel within to ensure that the innocent are protected, and that the sick & perverted are punished for their sins. They must face down whatever challenges confront them. They must be ready!

They must be able to *cope*.

And once they can *cope*, they can serve.

That's all I ask of them.

I glance around this disgusting living room, almost improved by the poisonous blood of the demonic deceased, and see the key difference within this crime scene compared to those that came before it.

Levy's killer has left an ominous message for the police.

You'll Never Find The Bodies

Hm.

So artistic, and yet so vulgar.

The message is true. I've known all along, at each property, despite what I was telling Mercer & Gates and the other colleagues I happened to briefly interact with. They've impressed me today, and a small part of me takes comfort knowing that they will hopefully develop the steel needed. They'll brace themselves, buckle up and crack on, working hard to solve all the cases that come their way in the years to come.

When it comes to this one, however, despite their best efforts, despite all their labour, there's one thing *I* know that *they* never will...

The bodies truly will never be found.

I made sure of that.

Aftermath

I sit here upon a rooftop overlooking the town. It is around 6am, and as the sun rises in the distant sky, creating a glow across the landscape, there is an eerie silence that consumes the air, only occasionally broken by the fluttering and hawking of birds. I wonder if they realise how different life is. There is no longer the hustle and bustle of human life dominating the land, instead now there is a new norm; quiet throughout the day, often briefly interrupted by shouting, arguing, brawling and gunshots. I hope what has survived of nature is enjoying the newfound peace and quiet, however long it lasts each day, or beyond all of this.

I'd like to think I prepared myself for this, albeit through a combination of two rather contrasting things.

The first was quite simple; trust nobody, suspect everybody, think the worst of the world, base yourself in realism & cynicism and expect that one day that the world would crumble to the state in which it has.

The second was more light-hearted, but probably to be expected given my social alienation; the sheer number of hours spent playing *Fallout*! Wandering the wasteland living off scraps, engaging in abstract warfare every day, wondering if you'll still be alive 24 hours from now, wondering whether all of this is worth it...

Indeed, I've slept in about thirteen different beds over the last few weeks. As much as I'd love to stay in one place on a permanent basis, occasionally venturing out to hunt and gather supplies, the state of the real-life wasteland we now live in makes it impossible to set up camp alone without soon allowing myself to be a target for gangs. I still maintain an inkling of hope that I can find a settlement of decent enough people in which I can put myself to good use, but so far there's been no luck.

For now, I am simply left to my own devices. And by that, I mean, keeping an eye on the town from this rooftop, planning a route to my next destination and ensuring I have enough to keep me going in the meantime. My defence mechanisms consist of a rifle, a pistol and some scrappily welded armour I've managed to put together over time during salvage-runs. For what it's worth, I've been quite proud of the job I did, especially considering the torso piece has managed to deflect more than a couple of bullets so far.

Although I said I believed I'd prepared myself for this life, I must contradict that somewhat by saying that, at the same time, I never believed I'd actually survive what I've faced so far. I never believed I'd be capable of holding my own when the raider gangs formed and made the most of anarchy, nor that I'd be able to live without anybody by my side. But that's what I've done so far... and so much more. I've had to. In this new world, the aftermath of the apocalypse, if you're "lucky" enough to have survived, then you get to play a new game; kill or be killed. Whereas before it was all about bruising your knees for the man in the suit, grafting and toiling day after day for the benefit of a society hellbent on making life unlivable, now it's about grafting and toiling for the benefit of existing.

For the benefit of seeing the decaying world for another day. For the benefit of pushing on to see whether there's anybody out there who is making as much of a fight of it as you are, and is willing to try and salvage something of this new world.

The apocalypse...

It's almost funny saying it like that. Using that old, demonic word. The word that signifies the end of days, the endgame for humanity...

Certainly, the apocalypse as we know it signified the endgame for human civilization as it was, and in a crude way, it's a good thing. Good riddance to the world that once was. A world of capital, of deviancy, of materialism, of strife. Long had humanity lost its way, too obsessed with intertwining with each other and searching for the ultimate thrill, the ultimate orgasm, the ultimate pleasure. Instead of touching the stars, we as a species went in completely the wrong direction, so deep in the fog and the mire that we had long forgotten who we were. Everything unique and special about the different races and peoples was lost in a sloppy desire for each tribe to be the same, all the little grey people of the world desiring the true diversity of humankind to be melted down in a pot and turned into a nu-human society, built on nothing. No past, no history, no identity, just a conglomerate of aimless slaves consuming the product and conflicting with each other, not knowing why and not knowing how to break the mould.

In the end, it's hard to say what actually acted as the bullet that put society as we knew it out of its misery.

Was it the outbreak of the supervirus that ripped the world to shreds? Or was it simply that the decay deep within the modern human core had done too much damage and that that core had simply crumbled, like a block of timber diseased by woodworm?

Personally, I can't help but feel that it was both.

Humanity was already dying, the supervirus was simply the thing that the human immune system couldn't fight, both literally and metaphorically. The usual human ignorance to the virus was present, albeit understandable given the historical deceit of the system. The media of course were too obsessed with the obscenity of reality TV, the excuse for music on show at awards ceremonies, or the latest conflict seen in the big cities in different parts of the world. And we all know that social conflict, or even terrorist attacks, were all part and parcel of living in a major city...

The virus had already killed over 2000 globally when its impact truly started to be felt outside of its country of origin. By that point, it had discretely entered the water system, and blissfully unaware carriers had been unknowingly infecting multiple areas (and thus other people) for weeks before their own symptoms began to show. By the time the devastating potential of the virus began to dawn on people, it was simply too late. Forgive me for sounding rather sick, but I actually embraced the idea of the outbreak weeks before it truly struck us as a nation. I know, I know, it sounds dreadful, but humanity deserved such a kick in the balls, and admittedly I found it quite desirable to be able to cop out of society through something that wouldn't be my own doing. I never had the nuts to end my own life (I probably would've done it already rather than face the new world), so what better way to escape the vile nature of life in the 21st Century than to fall victim to a global pandemic and be able to quietly succumb to it, before making my way into whatever comes after life.

After life...

Ha! Forgive me, I just find it ironic, considering the afterlife, when instead I'm here, dealing with the aftermath of the pandemic. Maybe it's punishment; hoping to be caught in the tidal wave of a global wipeout and instead being left to pick up the pieces. Or maybe it's a challenge; my life was going nowhere prior to the apocalypse, but here I am now, being made by the conflict I face each and every day.

Oh? Hang on...

The first signs of life of the day. A couple of raiders staggering around a few blocks away. Trying to walk off a hangover by the looks of things. I've actually spent many early mornings like this. Some people would use the opportunity to kill a few of the scumbags from a distance, acting like a vigilante while the remaining decent survivors try and push on. And while I'll admit the temptation to put an end to some of these scrotes has arisen once or twice, I instead find myself preferring to enjoy these quiet moments while I can. The likelihood is that I'll have to face a few of these raiders on my travels today, whether through bargaining for safe passage or simply by emptying a few shells into some of them to clear the way, and I'll deal with them when I have to. For now, however, I'll save what ammunition I have, and keep close watch of the areas below.

I'm quite a fair way away from what I used to call home, now. While early on I had no problems navigating my way through areas I knew well, as my travels have continued, I have found myself battling not only the raiders and my own mindset, but also my lack of knowledge regarding whatever location comes next. In the early days, I knew of perfect hiding spots, shelters to rest my head for the night and the ideal route to where I wanted to go. Now, however, I must learn on the go, which enforces me to use this time wisely, and put it to good use. While each morning I savour the majesty of the sunrise in the event that it may be my last, I also memorise the streets ahead and what I have noticed before I set off. Doing so has ensured my safety (for the most part) on numerous occasions thus far, and long may it continue.

Hmm...

Long may it continue? How intriguing. I find myself longing to survive. Am I only just realising that? Maybe this new world is indeed making something new of me. I once desired that life would have meaning & cause, and how ironic that in a world devoid of hope & happiness, I find myself wanting to fight on day after day trying to see if such things still exist. Maybe that fight was there all along. Maybe it was just regularly beaten down and buried by the world around me, given no opportunity to rise and flourish. Maybe I could've been an asset to people, and indeed the wider world, if only I had been given the opportunity...

Ah well. Such is life. Clearly, being an asset to the old world is something that never came about. But maybe, just maybe, I could be an asset to this world. The new world.

As I look back down to the streets, I see those two raiders again. They've been joined by two others, and typically they are arguing. When I'm on foot strolling the streets, this is usually the perfect opportunity to sneak by safely. Until, of course, they hear you and instantly start shooting at you like it's the wild west. To be fair, I don't think the wild west could compare to this. So far, it has usually ended in me taking a few more lives and looting them for ammo and supplies. Quite cold and ruthless when I think about it. I really struggled with that early on. Killing to survive, looting to carry on. Eventually it becomes second nature, but you have to be aware that you'll lose some of your humanity as a result. Which in turn makes me grateful for the newborn desire to bring a semblance of good to the new world. Maybe it's an exchange of sorts; sacrifice part of who you are as a means of discovering a part of who you wish to be, and in turn, the world will benefit.

Yes, I HAVE considered how ridiculous it all sounds.

BUT... I need that motivation, and this certainly helps. The raiders below continue arguing, so much so that the volume begins to increase. I faintly hear one of them accuse another of stealing his whiskey. Poor bastard. He must rely on it for fuel.

I look in a different direction, trying to see if I can catch a glimpse of any other signs of life emerging for the new day. Aside from a couple of birds floating through the air, I see nothing. How dull and monotonous this landscape would seem were it not for the sun's sweet gleam...

I rise to my feet, stretching out as I do. I bend back down to pick up my weapons and a bag containing a few essential supplies. Once I straighten up again, I glance back over to the raiders. There's a bit of pushing and shoving going on now.

Fight, fight, fight, fight...

I turn and clamber back through the hole in the roof, making my way towards the dropdown stairs that lead to the upstairs landing down from the loft of this old house. I make one last use of the lavatory, before descending to the living room. This house had been long abandoned before I arrived a couple of days ago, but the spirit of the family who lived here remains. As such, I have tried to treat it with as much respect as possible in the time I have been here. I made the effort to straighten picture frames, tidy the house up and so on and so forth. I'm aware that in the event of torrential rain, the hole in the roof will render these chores null and void, but I just hope that, wherever the family is, whatever may have become of them, that they are at peace and that they can take comfort in the knowledge that somebody was grateful for their home and wanted to show gratitude in the only way possible. After all, I did use the lavatory...

But now, my time here must end. My essentials are gathered, and it is time for me to depart. The primary goal, as ever, is to see the next sunrise, twenty-four hours from now. Beyond that, anything is a bonus. I might even be an asset to somebody, or something.

If you don't hear from me, carry on as if I never existed. It's better that way. It's one of the ways I've managed to survive, now I think about it.

I often find it's best to remember the good things in life when you are at your strongest, because the pain of remembering such things when you are at your weakest can be unbearable. And there's too much pain in this life to have to suffer anymore.

Anyway, I'm off. Maybe I'll bump into those raiders. I wonder if they've got any whiskey left over that I can loot.

Remember, the sunrise in twenty-four hours...

She Lost Her Voice

"She truly was incredible."

Two nurses, both in their forties, sat back in their chairs as they gazed at the computer screen, on which a concert from some eight years prior was playing.

They were on their break in a small, cramped staff room, roughly midway through a particularly long shift. Given the trauma of the work, a pleasant look back at the majestic talent on show in the video was a nice reprieve. Everything about it stirred such good memories. The music, the iconography, the spectacle.

And the superstar with the beautiful voice.

"My only regret," the first nurse continued, "was that I never saw her doing what she did best in person. I'm not sure I would've been able to compose myself."

"Likewise," the other agreed. "I never had myself down as much of an opera fan, but she was such a unique talent, and whenever she appeared on TV, you just had to pay attention."

The nurses each took sips of their coffee whilst continuing to watch the performance, almost succumbing to a state of hypnosis in the process. The first nurse set her cup down on the table before gently biting her bottom lip, almost in consideration of something, before turning back to her colleague. There was a dinginess about the staff room, and it almost captured the lingering sense of loss hanging over the nurses as they watched the superstar.

"Do you remember where you were when it happened?"

"When what happened?"

"It. You know... 'it.'"

"Oh... yes, I think I do."

The second nurse seemed to drift off momentarily once she realised what the other was getting at. Not a pleasant memory, all things considered, now she thought about it in hindsight. Certainly, one of those moments that lives with you. The old "where were you when..." cliché definitely applied to this particular memory.

"Well?" the other nurse probed. "Where were you?"

"Oh," her colleague replied, somewhat surprised. "I was at home with the husband. It was a quiet night, nothing particularly special going on, aside from the fact that I was off that week. We had finished our evening meal and were watching the news when it came through. I think it was more the trauma than anything else that made it a news item. Any other time and it could've been one of those moments where the singer is just ridiculed rotten by the press and the public."

"Agreed," the other nodded. "I said the same thing to my fella the night it happened. Were it just a band playing a gig and it happened and whatever, it would've been embarrassing for the singer in question but that would've been it. With her, though, it wasn't simply about the fact that it happened, it was the magnitude of the moment and everything that followed."

The second nurse nodded in agreement, and firmly gripped her mug of coffee in her hands, as though suppressing the shudder of a memory, as the warmth of the mug's content tried to bat away the cold that threatened to consume the nurse's mood.

"Have you ever seen the footage?" she asked, wincing as she did.

"No," the other answered, glancing back at the screen. "I suppose I should really. Not out of some perverse curiosity, more just to get it over and done with. It's always been one of those things I wanted to avoid. Ironic isn't it? Trying to avoid the emotional trauma of witnessing a moment like that given the job we do."

The footage in question was actually available amongst the suggested videos down the right-hand side of the screen. The incident itself had been referred to as many things, one of which had been used as the title for the video, 'The Moment of Tragedy.' As the concert that was playing approached its conclusion, the first nurse rested her hand on the mouse and began to scroll over to the video in question, glancing back at her colleague as the cursor fell atop the video tile.

"Are you ready?" she asked, softly.

Her colleague waited a moment before replying, as the dinginess present continued to wage war against the warmth that she tried to fill herself with. The coffee was good, but there was something disturbing about trying to drink away a seemingly spiritual dread.

"Yes," she eventually answered. "Go ahead."

The video began, and there the superstar stood in all her splendour. Divine in both appearance and talent, she held her audience's attention within the palms of her hands, palms she held out as she began to sing. The song in question was the classic known as 'Un Bel Di Vedremo,' which translates to "One fine day we'll see." Such cruel irony, an irony not lost on either nurse as the bodies of both were consumed by goosebumps. The camera panned to various audience members, some of whom were either simply in awe or had broken down in tears. They were in the presence of a generational talent living out her dream, and every single individual there was savouring the moment. But the nurses knew that the horrifying moment was slowly creeping up on them, and they both wondered how they would respond once it came. They didn't have long to find out.

As the song itself neared its four-minute mark, and the singer began to enact the great vocal crescendo, the electricity in the concert halls could be felt in the dingy staff room. The singer didn't just have those present captured in her palms, she had made the world her audience and she held the world in her arms. That was, until her voice, when it should've left the world in awe at its peak, simply gave way.

The noise that emanated from her was haunting, as was the look on the singer's face, as her open palms suddenly reached for her own throat. Even crueller was the fact that members of her backing band were so entranced in the performance that they had simply kept on playing, and so the haunting music became the soundtrack for what the world was witnessing.

The downfall of a superstar, who sunk to her knees.

"Turn it off."

The first nurse suddenly became aware again of where she was, and her head swung to look at her colleague.

"What?" she managed to blurt out.

"Please," her colleague whispered, "turn it off."

The second nurse was well aware of what came next, and the performance itself was all she had needed to see. She didn't wish to watch the beginning of the superstar's descent.

The first nurse acquiesced to her friend's wishes, and quickly closed the tab, abruptly ending the video in the process. Where magnificent music had previously been the only sound heard in the room, now silence reigned, until the second nurse's tiny sniffles began. The first nurse placed her right hand over her friend's left in support and comfort, and allowed her to weep before she could compose herself.

Eventually, once she was comfortable, the second nurse said "I don't want to watch what comes next. I've been haunted by the written detail of it for too long, I don't need to be haunted further by the footage."

"I agree," the other responded. Glancing at the clock, she said "We've got another five minutes left, have a glass of water before we go back."

The two of them rose and began to get themselves ready for the resumption of their shift, as they washed their brew cups and made sure the staff room was ready for whoever wished to use it next, with the recreational computer logged out to adhere to security procedures. The second nurse swigged a small glass of water down, and as the clock ticked down, she joined her colleague in exiting the room and beginning the walk down the corridor.

The corridor. The dinginess in the staff room had nothing on the corridor. Corridors in health-related facilities often carried a unique soulless nature. Hospital corridors are synonymous with the sound of clanking footsteps echoing off the walls and window panels as a lone individual makes their way from one department to another, often only accompanied, albeit momentarily, by a vending machine located halfway down the corridor itself. Corridors in doctors' surgeries are often intended to give a more local feel, with the old neutral carpet coating the floor and replacing the clanking of footsteps with more of a redundant thud, a thud that in the past was accompanied by a bell and a small, cheap tannoy from which a receptionist would call out for the next patient to make their way to whichever room they needed to be. Nowadays, in somewhat more technological times, the bell remains but the tone is slightly different and is now accompanied by a large screen that sits high up on one of the walls in the waiting room that patients keep an eye on to see whether their name appears next before they can see the doctor or nurse.

This corridor, however...

You would've thought that a mental facility would at least make the attempt to present itself as a place where the damaged can be at peace during their treatment rather than be left to rot. It's all well and good requesting that you call such a place a 'mental facility' rather than an asylum, but what's the point when the aesthetic still screams *Arkham*?

Nevertheless, the two nurses pushed on, grimacing as the surrounding features fed on their souls, souls that needed to be at their strongest in this environment. Neither of them said a word as they approached the location of their designated patients for this shift. Such a sad state of affairs, these patients found themselves in. Many of them mumbled and shuffled around incoherently, some didn't utter a sound, while others were simply locked in behind their eyes. One, however, seemed to be a tragic conglomerate of all of these. As the nurses reached the large room where the patients awaited them, they were able to allow two of their colleagues to depart for their own break, as they took over their duties.

Instantly, one gentleman named Alastair almost bounced his way towards the first nurse, eagerly displaying a napkin on which he had doodled an undefinable picture of some sorts. The nurse took the napkin from him, feigned appreciation and thanked him, which appeared to satisfy his enthusiasm and eagerness, as he turned and trotted his way back towards the settee, where a couple of other patients sat beside him. In feigning appreciation, the first nurse wasn't necessarily unappreciative of Alastair's gift, it was more that she had seen it many times before, and was simply playing her part in a regular routine in which the patient was convinced he had created a piece of artistic genius and wished to share it with his carers, who he appeared fond of.

To their credit, the nurses and the staff in general were, thankfully, rather fond of their patients, too. It was the least they could be. There were far too many sick and twisted tales of patients' lives being made a misery in places such as this. Given the rather vulgar aesthetic the facility possessed, the very least the staff could do is make the effort to combat that vulgarity with quality care for those condemned.

The first nurse took a moment to examine the doodle, almost wondering just what Alastair may have done with his life were it not for his... predicament. Would he have been creating genuine pieces of art that people everywhere could've appreciated? She turned her head to the second nurse who, after glancing around the room ensuring all was well, appeared fixated on one patient in particular.

"You can't lose sight of looking after everybody else, m'dear," the first nurse reminded her.

Slightly stung, but understanding where her friend was coming from, the second nurse replied "I'm not losing sight. I just lose a little bit of spirit every time I see her."

Letting out a weak sigh, the first nurse gave the other a gentle nudge and said "Tell you what, go and spend some time with her. I'll keep watch over everyone else. If there's any trouble, I know you'll be ready if you're needed, but just go and be with her."

"Are you sure?" the other replied.

"I'm sure, go on."

Appreciating the gesture, the second nurse wandered over to the patient in question, who was sat in a large, comfortable chair in the corner, with her feet off the ground ever so slightly, perched on a tiny, soft coated pouffe.

She appeared very much lost, maybe in a world only she was aware of behind her brilliant blue eyes. The woman wasn't a mute, but she very rarely made a sound, and even when she did, it was often a delicate mumble that could easily slip under the radar.

The nurse pulled up one of the comfy chairs so she could sit with her, offering a gentle smile as she did.

"Hi, Jeanie," she said softly as she sat down. "Everything okay?"

Jeanie's glazed eyes shuffled slightly in the direction of the nurse, seemingly only slightly aware of her presence but enough to realise that she wasn't alone. Once her senses stabilised somewhat, her mouth appeared to move somewhat, like that of a child learning to speak. Alas, however, as was often the case, no words emerged.

"It's okay, Jeanie," the nurse reassured her. Noticing an empty cup on a small wooden table beside her chair, she said "I hope your drink was nice."

Jeanie looked away momentarily, then her head seemed to shift in the direction of the cup, and the nurse thought she saw the woman give a nod as though to say 'Yes, it was nice,' though that may have simply been a tremor of sorts.

Jeanie's head rose and turned back in the nurse's direction, although her eyes only occasionally met those of the nurse and never for more than a fleeting moment. "You don't need to say a word, Jeanie," the nurse whispered. "I'm just going to stay here and keep you company."

For the briefest moment, the nurse could've sworn a smile was present on Jeanie's lips, but like the phantom nod, she couldn't be certain. Jeanie's left hand rose to her face, the nail of her thumb brushing over her lips, as she appeared to wish to say something, but ultimately, she couldn't. She then caught the eye of the nurse intentionally, who shared her gaze, gentle but firm so that Jeanie would know that they were silently sharing a moment. Jeanie's left hand then slipped slightly and the tips of her fingers rested on her collarbone momentarily, before she spread them in a gesture that made the nurse's heart sink.

Jeanie had delicately placed her fingers across her throat, and then slowly shook her head, in a displaying motion that told the nurse that she was trying to speak, that she was trying to communicate, but that she was simply unable to do so. Not properly anyway. The nurse responded by reaching out and taking the hand that Jeanie was gesturing with, and pulled it away, placing it in her other free hand and stroking it in a comforting manner.

"It's okay," she whispered again, holding back tears that threatened to burn her eyes. She was grateful that Jeanie had responded by simply turning her head to look out of the window while her hand was tendered to.

The nurse turned her own head to look back at her colleague and friend on the far side of the room, who also wore a look of heartbreak on her face. She, too, had seen the gesture that Jeanie had made, just as the two nurses had seen it earlier on during their break. The same gesture made by the superstar with the beautiful voice.

For Jeanie *was* the superstar with the beautiful voice. In the aftermath of her tragic breakdown on stage that the nurses had declined to watch any further, her life, and her mind, had simply fallen apart, to the point that there was no other place for her but here. Here, in this soulless place. Now, she was simply a gentle being who lived out her days making very little fuss and gathering very little attention, but those who knew her here in the asylum (sorry, "facility") knew of her story, and knew just how tragic it had been. She had brought joy to millions, and now her predicament broke the hearts of those she had brought joy to who had to bear witness to what she had become.

Jeanie, the superstar, who lost her voice, and lost her mind.

Fear In The Inn

The Summer of 2001.

How has it been so long?

I should really stop focusing on the time, but it's all so easy to be caught up in time. Time is inevitable, and yet in a way, despite its constant presence, almost unknowable.

And at its worst, a most cruel thing.

So much has changed, and yet it still feels like yesterday. Such a cliché, I know, but memories are like that, aren't they?

So near, yet so far, just over the bar.

But yes, The Summer of 2001.

And, in particular, a little village.

We were only in this little village for a week, but memories were made. I found out what love was that summer, in a funny kind of way.

It took us years to pronounce the name of the village properly, but no matter, we never get it wrong anymore. That village will live with us forever, regardless of whether we ever step foot in it ever again.

It's an old little place, roughly three miles from the coast. There's an old stone church site, a dinky little train station, an old corner shop that's now a convenience store and countless other little local outlets, one of which makes a killing selling firewood. There's a little DIY shop that has a CD rack, surprisingly enough. There's a chip shop that's quite decent, and a shop that sells retro toys that probably go for an arm and a leg on eBay.

We didn't stay in the centre of the village, itself.

No, we stayed at a little campsite down the road, and we used to walk into the village from there.

Morning paper and your bits for breakfast? Walk into the village to the corner shop!

Fish & Chips? Walk into the village to the chippy!

Fancy a pint on the first night? Walk into the village and head for the local!

And that's what we did.

In later years gone by we stayed in different parts of the village, almost forming a triangle of locations stayed when I think about it, but those same routines remained each time. Apart from the latter...

Anyway, back to the first time.

We took Bolan's advice and rode the white swan, and the first night of this little week away became arguably *the* most memorable. Or, at least, the first in a line of memorable days & nights.

It was a pleasant old inn, and while not jam packed, it was relatively busy, people gathered sipping pints and one or two here & there enjoying a bit of food. I was only young at the time, and nights like this were a rarity to me, so I found myself enjoying the setting, or at least the novelty of it. We found a little spot tucked in with a table, and food & drinks were ordered. As the orders were made, we seemed to become accustomed with the landlady of the premises and her husband. A boisterous lady, she was proud of her pub and the service she provided, and she was eager to get to know us, a small family from a fair ol' way away that had come to stay for the week. As the night progressed, she gave us as much of her time as possible, as we shared stories and what not, enjoying laughs and all the rest. Me being the youngster, she made a point of being fussy in her service, putting together an ice cream special which could only be described as divine.

She became almost like one of those protagonist aunties you see in stories, the ones often without kids who relieve a family of stress whenever they arrive. Either way, she was in her element, even more so when she offered haircuts.

Yes, a landlady offering haircuts.

And a haircut is what I got!

I was asked to join the landlady as she took me to a room in the back, the doorway to which was pretty much facing our table. She had a desk with a mirror there, almost like one of those old dressing room mirrors you see in theatres. While she remained ever positive, the room itself left a bit to be desired. Cold and stagnant, unlike the welcoming nature seen in the main area of the pub.

And then she left.

She needed to gather the necessary bits to cut hair, you know, scissors & combs and the like. But just like that, I was alone in this dingy backroom in a pub a good century's worth of miles away from home. Safe to say, I was left a bit uneasy. I had one of those curious minds anyway, even at that age, so it didn't take much for my mind to wander, but as is often the case with kids, baseless fears and curiosities are often just that; baseless. This would've appeared to be just another of those moments, but there was something... different.

The landlady had left the room via the door we had entered through, so she had simply returned to the main area of the pub to nip behind the bar itself to go through another door to fetch her necessities. I knew where *that* doorway led to.

But not the *other* doorway.

The doorway that stood behind me to my right, about two meters or so back. That day was where my mindset seemed to evolve from mere childlike curiosity and caution of the unknown to a genuine fear, as though prickled and poked by something unseen.

It was ajar, but nothing beyond it could be seen.

It was simply... black.

As though no light existed on the other side. Nothing could be seen; nothing could be heard. It was as though there was something unspeakable in the darkness. Its very existence bred fear, and that fear crept up on me like nothing I had experienced before.

I remained frozen in the chair in which I had been perched, and sat gazing into the mirror. I tried to focus strictly on my own reflection, watching the fear consume me as I did. Once or twice, I found myself looking back at the doorway, the blackness returning the glance.

And if thou gaze long into an abyss, the abyss will also gaze into thee.

Looking back almost felt like suicide.

Just don't look back at it, I remember thinking, *just look into the mirror.*

And yet...

And if thou gaze long into an abyss, the abyss will also gaze into thee.

What exactly was I supposed to do?

The landlady still hadn't returned, and my mind began to question the possibility of abandonment.

Silly, unquestionably, but this had gone beyond childish worries. This room, this inn, this fear.

None of this felt natural.

It felt like an eternity for her to return.

But return, she eventually did. As though nothing had been the matter, as though she hadn't been gone so long. Perhaps she hadn't. I didn't quite know what to think. I was simply relieved she had, indeed, returned. She cut my hair, and to her credit she did a damn good job!

Before you knew it, I was back at the table where I belonged, and we enjoyed the remainder of our night. So much so, in fact, that we stayed right till the end. Everybody else in the pub was gone by the time 2am rolled around, and yet we were still there. We eventually returned to the campsite in the dead of night, promising to return to the pub at the first opportunity.

The following day was a lazy one, as the elders found themselves strung up by hangovers while my young self came to terms with the enjoyment and the late-night shenanigans, whilst also being unable to rid my mind of thoughts of the backroom. I had managed to push aside any silly thoughts of the room once I had left it the previous night, but now such thoughts crept back up on me.

Thankfully, I was able to appreciate the outstanding summer weather, as the hours ticked by and the first full day of this short stay could be enjoyed.

Later in the day, we kept true to our word, returning to the inn full of eagerness built up from the previous night. What followed was arguably more adventurous, even if on the face of it, it seemed like a regular Saturday night in a pub.

The landlady was even more boisterous this time around, treating her audience to a karaoke night dressed to the bone in flamboyant costume, she and her husband welcoming us back with open arms in delight.

I'm glad to report that no such instances of isolation and abandonment in out-of-place rooms took place that night. In fact, this particular karaoke fest took place upstairs from the regular ground floor of the inn, before follow-up drinks were consumed in the latter area once the fun was over. Seeing more of the inn's layout made the dingy room feel even more out of place. How could a room seemingly touched by something indescribable and dark even exist in an inn so welcoming and warm?

But clearly it did have a place in that inn, though we never saw it again.

And by that, I mean, we never saw it again. The inn itself, not just the room. We never returned, for whatever reason. The landlady and her husband actually advised us on our first visit that they were in the process of leaving the inn and purchasing a new one on the coast I mentioned earlier, but we never got round to visiting them.

The rest of our week in that village was beautiful, only dampened by a sad end in which goodbyes were said and a soaking downpour seemed to symbolize our sadness at leaving. We returned the following summer to that particular campsite, then again to a different location some seven years later, then to a cottage a further five years later (thus completing the triangle) in which we stayed a second time a further two and a half years after that.

But the inn... we never stepped foot in the inn again.

We always said we would, but we never did. Something just seemed to prevent us from doing so. It seemed so perfect; the quaint village with its welcoming locals (in the summer at least, a little drab in the winter), unique little shops and idyllic character.

The inn sat perfectly, pretty much in the centre of the village. We walked past it each time we were there, but never stepped inside. I wonder now whether my parents had been affected by it as I was.

You see, those two nights were amazing. Memorable, fun and always great to look back on in conversation, and yet something stopped us from going back. Some might say it was just a desire to prevent those memories from being tarnished somewhat. After all, the landlady and her husband wouldn't even have been there in the second year we stayed in the village, let alone any years since. But... I don't know.

Then I remember a... dream, of sorts. No, not a dream.

A nightmare.

Only brief, and yet it still lives with me.

A dream that could only have come about had I seen more of the inn, as we did on the second night.

In it, we found ourselves in the inn in the dead of night, a dark blue tint affecting the light, only blemished somewhat by streetlights creeping through the boarded-up windows. An invisible horror was in possession of the inn, and a horrifying aura was present throughout, as though the character of that small, dingy room was reflected upon the entire premises. Or, as though the character of that room was the true nature of the inn, and as though the welcoming vibe the rest of the place exuded was simply a façade.

We had found ourselves upstairs, where the karaoke had taken place, but all I recall was running down those stairs to escape to the outside world. Even then, as we reached the ground floor, the invisible horror seemed to be riding on our shoulders, and we desperately tumbled over each other, desperate to get out!

And then out we were.

Safe, secure, and away from the horrors.

On reflection, those horrors have never left me, yet I don't even know what they were. Maybe there's a reason the landlady and her husband sold the place and left. Maybe their warm hearts and generosity were their attempts to beat back the inn's cruel persona. Maybe they had done all they could, and simply had to leave it behind, unable to penetrate the darkness any further.

And maybe that's the reason we never went back.

Maybe, without even knowing it, we simply knew we couldn't return. Or maybe, the inn itself was keeping us at bay. It didn't need to consume us on our return, it had already left its mark. We adored it, despite its malevolence. We adored it not knowing of its true nature, and as such, it had won.

Or maybe, this is all just foolishness, no different to that of a child when he or she thinks a bit too much.

Either way, I'm not sure I've ever been the same since...

The Slaughter Man

The family of three; Father, Mother and the Son. How they ended up here is somewhat of a blur, but here they are, nonetheless, in an old, nailed-down caravan on an off-road water-facing park off the back of an industrial estate, buried in the trees. You'd be forgiven for not knowing of its existence, nor even suspecting that such a little place could exist in such a location. Just beyond the trees lies a train station, and you can be almost certain that the majority of the passengers who have been on the trains that have hammered by over the years also have no idea that the park is there.

But many have stayed in this old caravan, and while the caravan itself may not be very unique, the place in which it is located certainly is. There is an aura about it, the water bringing calm yet leaving one with a world of questions & suspicions. A nearby greenhouse almost presented like a local information desk. A large fountain in the middle of the park, albeit one that hasn't had water run through it for many years. Ironic, given the abundance of water nearby. And on the other side of the park, a walkway that the family began to embark on when they arrived, but decided against it and have never returned to.

It is July, and the weather has consistently fluctuated from a skin burning blaze in the daytime to a window-bashing monsoon at night. On this particular occasion, it is the latter, and while usually the family jovially enjoys the experience of hearing the wind & the rain peltering the caravan they are staying in, tonight there is a lingering darkness affecting the collective mood. Tonight, you see, is the last night of their brief reprieve from society, and in the morning, they will gather their things and drive the one hundred or so miles home. Perhaps it is the knowledge that their time away is coming to an end that is affecting their demeanor, as they prepare themselves for everything the world back home has to throw at them. It is a summer of great change for the family, despite not much seemingly happening, and when they return, they will only have a matter of weeks to ready themselves for the beginning of a new chapter in the story of life.

That has to be it. Just the world back home, lingering over them like a philosophical shadow in contrast to their peculiar enjoyment of the real darkness of the night's wind and rain.

The u-shaped nature of a static caravan settee allowed the three of them their own space to put their feet up and drift off into the atmosphere, but there seemed to be a mutual understanding, albeit a silent one, amongst the family that there was an air of uncertainty afflicting them.

The son is the first to break the silence, doing so with a heavy sigh, before saying "Only a few hours left. It's been a nice little break, though, hey..."

His parents nod in agreement; a hint of somberness clear in their faces.

This brief reprieve hasn't been entirely without problems, as evidenced by a call from back home which caused a great deal of stress and anger. In addition to that, pre-existing anxieties have afflicted this family throughout this holiday.

The Son is plagued by the struggles of the last two years while coming to terms with the end of a certain chapter in his life. The Father is weighed down heavily by work requirements, the nature of his duties contrasting heavily with the level of toll his body is able to withstand, the character of his colleagues contrasting unpleasantly with his own.

The Mother, meanwhile, remains the emotional rock of this household, as has been the case for so long and will probably remain so for some time. To her credit, she does not allow her own struggles to show, but for how long she will be able to continue doing so remains to be seen.

As they each sit and quietly ponder life, the Son considers the minor events of the holiday thus far. Being sunburnt by the water very early on, hearing of a pathetic collapse in the cricket roughly midway through, receiving an aberration of a haircut in one of the nearby towns. This spell away represents the first for the family in three years, and as is often the case with holidays for this family, it has been uniquely charismatic in its own way. Regardless, the Son gazes out through the rain-soaked window, looking out across the park towards the greenhouse. He wonders about the park's past, whether it was more prosperous at one point prior to being hidden behind the industrial estate, and in doing so, he wonders what the future has in store for the park. Was its survival in question? Would people still have somewhere to come? And what about those who reside here permanently, such as the old bugger constantly asking if you need a day ticket, and the other bloke...

Ah, yes. The other bloke.

The Slaughter Man.

I bet his dreams are haunted by the cries of animals...

He actually seems to be quite a decent fella. Down to Earth, keeps to himself, says "Hello" cheerfully enough whenever seen, and just goes about his business. But a Slaughter Man is a Slaughter Man all the same, and one can never truly feel comfortable in the company of a man whose fingernails permanently wear the blood of his victims, regardless of whether his victims are human or animal. He actually lives in the caravan next door to this one. The close proximity itself to such a man, despite his demeanour, causes a shiver to run through the Son.

Or maybe it's just the cold night, the rain almost soaking his psyche just as it soaked the exterior of the caravan. Funny how the weather can impact one's mood in such a way. The sunshine almost birthing a fresh smile, the rain almost inducing tears to fall from one's eyes.

After all, why be so silly as to succumb to baseless fears that a man who slaughters animals for a living could actually be tempted to butcher some human meat for a change? Even just as a hobby on the side? Silly indeed...

"Shame to be leaving early," the Father says suddenly. "All just to go back and face those bastards back there. You get away from it only to be pulled back in, and wrongly as well!"

"Just don't think about it," the Mother replies soothingly. "You'll deal with it in a couple of days when we're back home. Until then, just enjoy the last few hours we've got away from it all."

Stress, worry and concern; a collective dead weight around the neck of human existence. Existence itself is so often tainted with woe, that the added factor of painful anxieties, brought about usually by the social condition, only add further misery to the lifespan of an individual, in addition to their loved ones. As such, the Son finds himself questioning not only his social condition, but his mental state as a whole. He sees his family consumed by a collective depression, worsened heavily by the actions of his Father's work colleagues, further compounded by the weight the Son himself carries from his years on Earth thus far, further impacted by the Father and Son's combined guilt that the Mother has to carry the burden of their woes and anxieties. This collective and individual depression is met head-on by a petty paranoia centered around an innocent gentleman who has only presented a show of decency whenever encountered. To actually, albeit without malicious intent, have manifested the idea that the man may decide he'll not let the family return home any time soon, that instead he'll be scratching his slaughter equipment across the caravan's outer walls in preparation...

Madness. Insanity. Foolishness.

Pathetic.

That's how the Son feels, as he realises that the Slaughter Man is not a real threat to his or his parents' lives, but is instead reflective of a deeper, inner threat; the threat his own fragile mind poses to his own existence and to his future. The Slaughter Man is not a genuine threat that will burst through the caravan doors and leave a bloody mess of the family on their final night here. The false fear he instigates is instead sprung from a mite-like threat that worms its way around the brain of the Son, slowly but surely decaying his mind, birthed by the youngster's experiences that he will carry for all his remaining years, however many he will have. The constant fear that something or someone will bring pain and misery to him and his family, the constant belief that they will surely never know happiness... that is the true reflection of the Slaughter Man that exists in the world behind the Son's eyes.

Petty. Foolish.

And all in all, quite unfortunate.

And so, the Son finds himself imagining he is outside, being bathed by the rain as though he is bathing in shame, almost oblivious as ever that his vivid imagination is dictating the direction of his thought patterns, succumbing as ever to visions of a contrasting nature; thematically dark, colourfully descriptive.

It is that vivid imagination, complete with thematic contrasts, overt focus on the past, bludgeoning fear of the future, and overall fatigue of life as a whole, that he carries with him as the family soon says goodnight and splits into their respective bedrooms. It is that vivid imagination that works tirelessly in his mind, doing unpaid overtime, while his eyes lie shut despite his mind's eye being fully alert. The vivid imagination that keeps him awake until his body eventually adheres to Mother Nature and simply cannot allow him to remain awake any longer, as he eventually succumbs to sleep.

Somewhere nearby, meanwhile, a scratching begins, like the sound of sharp tools slowly grinding along the side of a caravan, discrete at first but gradually increasing, as though the caravan itself is being used to sharpen blades in preparation for slaughter.

Whether these sounds are the last echoes of the Son's mind before he falls *asleep*, or the first echoes of the sounds of his *dreams*, he isn't entirely sure, nor is he sure of what's real anymore...

Stroll Down An Irish Road

This is the tale of a young English family that travelled to the Emerald Isle and never came home.

Sometime in the Summer of 2003, after months of anticipation, this young family, having packed their bags in preparation, set off under the shadow of darkness in the very early morning.

Travelling by car, they jumped onto the motorway and made their way to a sea port in the Welsh town of Holyhead, where twelve months earlier they had parked their car and boarded a ferry to the Northern Irish capital of Belfast. That particular occasion had been a solitary day out; a trip across the sea and a few hours enjoying a taster of the famed Irish way of life. It had whetted the family's appetite, and they immediately fell in love with the country, promising to themselves that they would return at the earliest convenient moment.

Fast forward twelve months, and that convenient moment had arrived. This time, however, they took the car with them, arriving at the sea port with plenty of time to spare, allowing them to comfortably drive into the basement-like car park aboard the ferry, thus allowing them to ascend to the more socially atmospheric area aboard the vessel. Once settled in, they enjoyed drinks and snacks as the ferry set sail to its destination. As the journey progressed, the family would occasionally step outside to enjoy the lung engulfing winds that blew by as they sailed the sea, gazing across the ocean with great admiration as they grew ever closer to the start of their holiday.

On the conclusion of the journey, they again arrived in Belfast, though only temporarily in contrast to the previous summer. Whereas on their day out last time they had specifically wandered the city, this time around they quickly departed the capital in order to reach their chosen place of stay; County Fermanagh. More specifically, they would be residing in the little village of Tulleyhommon that uniquely neighbours the village of Pettigo that falls within County Donegal of the Irish Republic. They would effectively be staying almost literally on the Irish Border.

Waiting for them was a semi-detached bungalow that sat on a row of semi-detached bungalows, that almost seemed to spring out of the middle of nowhere once reached as you drove down the road towards them. The border line was almost immediately to the left of the bungalows as you came off the street that played host to them, while the village of Kesh lay to the right, albeit roughly four miles away, while roughly a mile back behind the bungalows lay an almost silent stretch of water beyond a discrete stretch of road coated by trees that could probably tell a thousand stories. Somewhat humorously, the street that hosted the bungalows also had something of a garden of its own that lay between the bungalows and the main road, where a platoon of sheep would wander around seemingly occupied by conversation a human could never understand, interrupted only by the occasional meal. One poor sheep in particular had bollocks the size of swollen, misshaped melons, which caused a considerable amount of emotional pain to any gentleman who happened to bear witness to such an uncomfortable sight, though god only knows how that kind of pain contrasted with whatever the sheep was experiencing. He didn't seem to show any obvious signs of discomfort, bizarrely enough; instead, he simply just went about his business alongside his fellow kind, almost in acknowledgement that he was part of the furniture in this seemingly magical little place.

The family arrived in a joyous mood, and they were welcomed warmly by the locals, particularly by the woman in the bungalow neighbouring their own which wasn't directly connected. Intriguingly enough, the bungalow that *was* attached to theirs was empty, and while nothing was ever said about it, there was undoubtedly a slightly disconcerting sense of peculiarity about that empty property. Regardless, the family quickly settled into their temporary residence, eagerly looking forward to the many memories that would undoubtedly be made over the next fortnight.

The location contrasted so heavily with home.

Waking up in the morning to near silence, with the only sounds emanating from the aforementioned sheep, or a twittering bird, or (unfortunately, albeit rarely) a passing truck that was driving by to either enter the Republic or return from it. Mornings were steady, with breakfast enjoyed in a simple yet cozy kitchen that was all-in-one with the living room. The radio provided the setting for the day, informing the listeners of local news, weather and sport, the latter in particular of great importance given the ongoing All-Ireland Series as well as the great interest in the soon-to-begin 2003/04 Premiership season back home. Indeed, though Irish interest in English football was common knowledge, it was still intriguing for the family to witness the enthusiasm first hand, alongside their own enthusiasm for the All-Ireland Series. Conversations were had with the temporary neighbours regarding both sporting events, which only added to the sense of welcoming the family had experienced in addition to their general settling in. Often it is the case where new arrivals in any country completely fail to even attempt to assimilate with the local and national cultures, though on some occasions some new arrivals actually embrace the cultures with great enthusiasm and in turn end up irritating the locals. Thankfully, the family had struck the perfect balance in showing both intrigue and appreciation; the ideal visitors.

They didn't simply remain in the bungalow, of course. They spent their days visiting various locations both in Northern Ireland and in the Republic, such as Derry and the Giant's Causeway in the former, and Bundoran in County Donegal in the latter. These days were filled with laughs and good times, accompanied by sight-seeing and picture taking, with mementos of various kinds purchased from each, such as sporting items, fridge magnets, flags and so on.

There were, however, two particular occasions where trips out left somewhat of a sour taste in the collective mouths of the family.

The first came early on in the holiday, when the family decided to step over the border to visit an idyllic little pub in Pettigo. Both aesthetically and atmospherically, the pub was like something from a bygone age. It seemed to wear a soul all of its own, almost carrying dark bags under its eyes yet retaining a true sense of individual beauty. Its patrons sat at the bar, possibly feeling as though this place could be their second home.

For the English family, however, the atmosphere carried a darkly unwelcoming tone. They had quietly mentioned to each other on the walk from Tulleyhommon that the local landscape seemed to have a life of its own, and those vibes had only strengthened once they reached Pettigo. Having settled down in the pub, they instantly knew that their presence was an issue for the locals. Not that anything was openly said by either the family or the locals. After all, their English coins were being chucked into the pub's coffers, so they had the right to enjoy their drinks and be left in peace. But they were English, and regardless of how they felt about past events, regardless of how much money they spent in this pub, and regardless of how much love they had for Ireland, they were simply not wanted here.

To their credit, the family could appreciate the attitudes of the locals, even if it left them uncomfortable. They knew full well of the troubles of the past, and of the attitudes many Irish men and women carried towards the English, even by those who ironically found themselves living and working in England. Although probably naïve, the family found themselves in the category of people who took pride in their own identity and heritage whilst greatly admiring those features within the Irish peoples, and thus hoped that the pain of the past could be left behind as new friendships blossomed. They remained in the pub for barely an hour, before reluctantly accepting the situation and heading back to the bungalow. There were no incidents, especially as the pub was only around ten percent full, but the atmosphere alone was enough for them to depart and never return. The bartender's blunt demeanour and dialogue, the regular glances and dirty looks, the soft yet spiteful mutterings...

The message had been received oh so quietly, and yet oh so loud and clear; no English welcome around here.

The experience certainly left a dampener on that particular evening, especially in the minds of the younger members of the family who, though vaguely aware of the troubles, had no real idea of the finer details nor of their long-term impact. To those younger members, Ireland was a beautiful place full of beautiful people, and that appreciation was something they believed would be mutual. Encountering people who wouldn't even bother to piss on the family if it burned in flames was a harsh reality check. But it lacked in impact in contrast to the second unpleasant occasion.

This second occasion was somewhat bizarre in its happenstance, in that it occurred completely accidentally and yet for the majority of the time during it, the family failed to realise the severity of their situation. They had taken another trip to Belfast, as they had the year before, and had for the most part been enjoying their day out. When the time came to return to their car, however, they suddenly found themselves lost, and took a plunge in deciding what direction they would take to get back to the vehicle and thus the bungalow. In doing so, they drifted rather aimlessly, and found themselves in the midst of what they would discover was a "Catholic part of Belfast." A somewhat foolish description it would seem, especially given that the city centre could hardly be deemed the "Protestant part of Belfast," but it would become clear that the particular area they had drifted into was more Irish-Catholic centric, and thus viewed as somewhat of a no-go zone for any poxy English tourists. The family were openly talking amongst themselves when they came across an Irish gentleman, possibly in his fifties or so and casually intoxicated. More fortunately, he had a guardian's mentality that day, as he stopped the family and took the father to one side. Leaving the other members of the family a couple of metres away to chat amongst themselves as they glanced around their surroundings, the father and the local engaged in discussion for roughly twenty minutes or so, after which they shook hands and said their goodbyes. Upon returning to his family, the father wore a disturbed look as he quietly, in no uncertain terms, told his family not to say a single word and turn back the way they came and return to Belfast city centre, where they would hopefully be able to find the car.

It was during this silent walk back that the youngsters truly began to develop a fear, not simply of potentially unwelcoming locals, but of Ireland as a whole. And by Ireland, one means the island of Ireland as a single nation as visualized by the Republicans. The idea of Northern Ireland and the Republic of Ireland being viewed as separate entities quickly evaporated in the minds of the youngsters. It became clear that despite the affection that they shared with their parents for the Irish culture and people, there was a heavy anti-English sentiment still present either side of the border that the youngsters had known nothing about, and discovering it scared them. Why would they carry such affection for a nation and its people if those things hated them in return? It would be like cuddling a childhood teddy only to discover your Mother had laced it with cyanide.

Once the father felt comfortable allowing his family to speak, the family unsurprisingly had an abundance of questions, but the father advised them to save them until they were comfortable.

Once back at the bungalow, the questions flowed, although even then the father advised them to watch the volume of their voices, lest any of the neighbours hear of what had happened.

That particular request left further doubt in the minds of the youngsters. These neighbours had been kind and welcoming; was the father saying that even *they* couldn't be trusted? Very quickly, all the goodwill and affection felt like lies, like a chocolate castle built on a foundation of lava.

It transpired that the gentleman who had spoken to the father had no qualms admitting his own historical distaste for all things English, particularly the people, but whether age or the alcohol had watered down his hatred couldn't be determined. Regardless, the man had felt the urge to inform the family, clearly carrying no malice within them, that they were entering a loose equivalent of no man's land, and he had duly given the father a short history lesson of the area. Should the family have come across the wrong people, with their English accents clear to any healthy ears, then... well, the insinuation was obvious. Regardless of the family's innocence, they would've been guilty simply of being the wrong people in the wrong place at the wrong time. The man had apparently wished the father and his family all the very best, and had even declared his own wish for better relations between the Irish and the English, despite his own prejudices. It was these departing words that the father placed emphasis on when talking to his children, as he made a firm point of reminding them that not all Irish folk carried such hate in their hearts, and even those that did were at least partially justified in doing so, regardless of his own English pride. Unfortunately for him, his attempts at comfort and guidance fell mostly on deaf ears, as the youngsters found themselves struggling to sleep that night whilst desperately wanting to return home as soon as possible.

Recognising his family's discomfort, the father made a point of localizing the holiday from that day onward, abandoning any plans he had to drive out deep into either the Northern nation or the Republic. In doing so, he hoped the family could allow themselves to again appreciate the beauty of the land and find themselves enjoying the local spirit that could be felt. It was a difficult endeavour, especially as the events of both Pettigo and Belfast had not only impacted his children, but also his wife. She was sturdy enough to ensure she didn't succumb to any of the fears her children were experiencing, but she couldn't deny that her enthusiasm had been blunted by the experiences, compounded by the newfound fears she had for her children's psychological welfare.

For the first couple of days after Belfast, the family never stepped foot off the street, remaining instead either in the bungalow or venturing into the back garden to enjoy some football or casual outdoor relaxation. They enjoyed their meals, drank lemonade purchased from a local supermarket and silently made a point of not mentioning what had occurred in the capital.

After those couple of days, the family set off to do some extra food shopping at the aforementioned supermarket, and on the way back through Kesh the father made a verbal point of noticing the Mayfly Inn, a gorgeous pub set in the village. He had intended to take the family there anyway prior to the recent events, but now seemed like a perfect time to nudge the family in the right direction. A night in a more accepting and social pub in a vibrant, pleasant and friendly village seemed the perfect opportunity to get the holiday back on track, even if the other plans for venturing across the country had been abandoned.

Much to his delight, the family collectively gave their approval, though he couldn't help but wonder whether the children were saying "yes" simply out of a sense of duty to their father, as a means of hoping to ensure he was able to enjoy the holiday he had hoped for.

Either way, plans were made, and as the family sat around the table that night enjoying their meals, they all declared their enthusiasm for taking a trip into Kesh twenty-four hours later.

The following morning began quietly, as the family took their time getting up, fully intending to relax in and around the bungalow for the majority of the day before heading off in the evening. The children again played in the back garden, as the parents sat watching them in loving amusement, though as they did, the father again found himself being tugged by guilt. Yes, the family had been somewhat reinvigorated since Belfast, but the fact that he had needed to shift course so dramatically left a heavy burden on his heart. He took great pride in not only his love for his family, but also the manner in which he led them as any man would wish to. Their distress was almost contagious, and though he possessed the ability to hide it from them, he was certainly distracted by the fears they found themselves afflicted by. Thankfully, however, he was able to push his quiet discontent away for the time being, as the youngsters had clearly succeeded in doing as they played, while his wife also seemed much more relaxed. That was all he could ask for; his family happy and at peace.

The hours eventually ticked by, and the family prepared themselves to depart to Kesh. With the parents very much intending to enjoy an alcoholic beverage or two, they called for a taxi to take them there, with the intent of returning back to the bungalow via that same method later in the evening. They were picked up around 6pm, and arrived at the Mayfly Inn a short while later. Once there, they settled themselves in around a table in a nice little spot in the corner of the inn, and ordered food and drinks from very friendly service staff. The positive vibes given off by the staff instantly put the youngsters at ease, which in turn instantly eased the minds of their parents. With all members of the family in a good place, both literally and metaphorically, they were able to properly enjoy themselves for the first time in a few days. Times like these were exactly what they had in mind prior to their voyage over the sea, and it was bliss to be so at ease.

As the hours continued to pass, the parents had consumed about three drinks each, while the youngsters had had their fair share of good food and pop. They found themselves enjoying their trip out so much that they had lost track of time, and so were taken aback somewhat when they realised they had been in the inn for about four hours. Caught somewhere between startled and amused, the family thanked the staff for their excellent service, and stepped outside to use a nearby phone box to order a return taxi.

There remained some light in the night sky, as was often the case in the summer, but given that it was around 10:30 on an early-August night, any light that did linger wouldn't be able to do so for much longer. It wasn't cold, thankfully, though there did seem to be a peculiar breeze beginning to blow by. A gentle breeze, it should be emphasised, but a breeze all the same. While the father kept the children occupied with some silly humour, his wife rang the taxi firm to organise their return to the bungalow. To his concern, however, her face appeared to show some frustration, as well as a hint of alarm. After five minutes or so on the phone, she stepped out of the phone box, and proceeded to provide her family with some disturbing news.

There wouldn't be a taxi ride home. The firm that had provided their travel into Kesh had suddenly found themselves without enough drivers to adhere to the family's needs, and unless they were willing to wait until after midnight for the rota to shuffle around enough to provide them with the transport they required, they were stuck.

The mother did her best to remain calm, especially to keep her children from getting themselves worked up, but her husband knew her well enough to recognise her frustration. Whatever had been said to her on the phone had clearly not convinced her that there was a genuine lack of drivers available to them. Maybe the individual on the other end of the phone *was* genuine, and simply had a poor way of expressing it, but the wife wore a look that said a thousand words, when all she really needed was one; doubt.

And doubt bred worry, and worry bred fear.

With that, the family was left with no choice, much to the angst of the youngsters. They would need to begin walking the four miles home back to Tulleyhommon, back to the bungalow.

The children were in disbelief, more out of a sense of the idea of walking through a place they barely knew at what could be a potentially unpleasant time, especially as they recognised the concern across their mother's face. But despite their youthful, confused protests, they had little option but to begin the stroll alongside their parents. As he had done while they waited outside the phone box, the father resorted to comic relief as a means of putting his family's minds at ease, and to some degree it worked, albeit inducing a heavy sense of cynicism within his offspring that he wasn't entirely sure existed previously. The general vibe the family carried was "this could only happen to us! Ah well, at least we can laugh about it later, a proper holiday tale…"

At least the stroll began with a collective smile.

Alas, it didn't last for long, as the light that had lingered in the skies earlier quickly evaporated, leaving the family under the dead of dark far sooner than they had anticipated. They were provided with a small reprieve however, as they approached a SPAR that sat just off the main road roughly twenty-five minutes or so from Kesh. Sensing an opportunity to gather some supplies for the walk, the family stepped inside and made a point of purchasing a torch for precautionary reasons and a couple of bottles of water to maintain their energies. Additionally, they tried to gather some extra information from the shop staff regarding travel arrangements, such as alternative taxi firms and what not, but the young women who were on shift were unable to aid them any further beyond accepting payment for the supplies. Irritated, the parents departed the shop somewhat abruptly, as they and their children resumed their walk. Accepting the likelihood of no transport being found to bail them out from this trek, they continued on up the road, hoping to hold on to whatever positive vibes they had managed to retain since their time in the inn. Those vibes, too, were soon lost.

While the road so far had been well lit with a walkway on either side, they quickly found themselves on a section of the road that seemed to leave civilisation behind somewhat. It should've been obvious to them, especially as the road they saw ahead of them now visually appeared very similar to the one in which the street of bungalows fell just off.

No walkways, no off-road premises such as shops or even houses, and quite alarmingly, very few street lamps.

Buying a torch suddenly seemed like a masterstroke, though the family hadn't anticipated the number of street lamps becoming so limited.

If they were enjoying any mild ego trip however as a result of buying the torch, that trip soon came to an abrupt halt, and any ego they possessed was soon deflated and kicked into the bushes alongside them, bushes that seemed to get larger with every meter they treaded.

The batteries that came with the torch had a life span even a fly would be ashamed of, and to make matters worse, the family hadn't considered buying a replacement pack. What had seemed like a mildly stressful stroll down an Irish road had suddenly become a late-night wander through hell's garden. On top of this, they had no means of knowing what time it was. The parents briefly nattered at each other regarding whether waiting until midnight for the next batch of available taxis should've been considered, nattering that came to a sudden halt when they approached the possibility that the firm may indeed have been lying to them. The potential for further worrying their children was too high, and the last thing the youngsters needed was to see their parents succumbing to such concerns, especially if their young minds were quickly becoming overwhelmed by their own fears and manifestations.

Fatigue was quickly setting in for all of them, and they could only guess how long they had been walking. Despite their collective desires to pause every once in a while, there seemed to be an unspoken agreement to simply keep on walking. The more they walked, the further they got, and the further they got, the closer they would be to the bungalow and thus to safety. The water, at least, had provided a source of fuel for them.

As they walked, each member of the family found their minds stirring over different concerns, some of which were shared amongst each other, not that they knew it.

The most obvious fears drifted back to those that had developed over the past week or so, brought about by the pub in Pettigo and the happenstance in Belfast. The mere term, "The Troubles," rang through the minds of each family member. An English family on Irish soil, wandering down a dark road, there to be picked off? The script cruelly wrote itself, and the inner monologues of the family members were reading it in silence as they walked.

Then there was the issue of local wildlife. They were hardly wandering through a jungle, but while a wildlife attack was highly unlikely, this holiday had already thrown up its fair share of surprises, this night being one of them! Admittedly, a distressed mind can stew over the pettiest of things, but the level of pettiness doesn't prevent it from being stewed over, regardless.

There was also the bog-standard threat of a drive-by assault. Troubles or no Troubles, a lost family could easily be ambushed on a road like this, whether by a basic scab in a small vehicle or a truck driver doing the overnight shift. Dark thoughts, indeed, but dark nights combined with dark occurrences tend to create dark thoughts, and potentially dark results.

In the midst of all these dark fears and concerns, a simple sense of innocence arguably stood out the most. It was something each family member possessed, but particularly the youngsters. The simple desire to get home. And not simply the bungalow, but *home*. The desire had only grown since Belfast, and while they had managed to press on and be as positive as possible, the youngsters' enthusiasm for the Emerald Isle had almost completely disintegrated. They weren't welcome here, they weren't wanted here and quite frankly, they didn't want to be here, especially not on this morbidly disturbing road in the middle of the night. The fear that they may never return home, for whatever reason, was the strongest thing that ran through their minds. Their lives had only just begun; they certainly wouldn't want them to end *here* of all places!

To the parents' credit, they had regularly provided comfort to their children, often only silently, with a little squeeze on the shoulders or what have you.

They seemed to have walked for an age, and with no sign of where they were, no idea of the time, and the consistent danger of evading passing cars whilst avoiding falling into the bushes looming over them, the family found themselves at arguably their lowest ebb of the holiday. The Father in particular was now truly wracked with guilt. Not simply tugged by it, as he had been earlier in the day when his family were in a far better place, but utterly wracked by it. It consumed him with every step he took, with every breath he exhaled, and with every thought in his head that he paid attention to.

It was *he* that had fed the enthusiasm his family had for this place, and if anything happened to his family, the thing he cherished most above all else, then even in death, he would never, ever be able to forgive himself.

Even this night, if nothing of any severity transpired, would leave a scar on the souls of his loved ones. A scar that would heal with ease and in no time at all, of course, but a scar that could've easily been avoided.

He didn't even need to drink! *He* could've played the role of taxi driver! *He* could've taken the family out, enjoyed the evening and then safely guided them home! If he really needed a drink, he could've bought one from that SPAR on the way home and dived into it once everybody was safely through the door of the bungalow with their shoes off and bums on the couch!

But no, instead they were here, in the dark, strolling down an Irish road, with their futures unforeseeable.

And then, as they carried on aimlessly, a car pulled up beside them…

***

What happened next cannot be detailed, for it is simply unknown.

One hopes to think that nothing horrific happened! The driver of the car may simply have offered them what they desired; a lift back to the bungalow. Safety and solitude captured in a short ride back to their beds, where they could sleep sweet dreams and put this night behind them. Once they awoke, maybe the experience had had an alternative effect on them. Maybe, in the days after, they decided to stay there for good. They had dreams after all prior to setting sail, and maybe the stresses of their experiences had actually strengthened their resolve. Maybe the goodwill of their saviour had reminded them that there was far more good than bad in the Emerald Isle, and that had in turn reignited their love for it. Maybe they're fine, and remain so to this day, and as such would chuckle at this tale.

Or maybe not.

Regardless, the truth indeed remains unknown…

Redeemed

"Forgive me Lord, for I have sinned."

A frail, scarred man, barely approaching his mid-thirties, kneels in the gravel and the dirt as he looks out across the stars.

In looking up above him, he hopes with all his will that his voice be heard by the one he worships the most.

And he begins his prayer, as the supposed sin he has committed is the thing that has brought him here, and he is due to give his final statement.

> *"This life I have known, has not been kind to me.*
> *The demons have consumed me, and their list of victories*
> *goes way beyond the scars on my body.*
> *The scars I have inflicted to rid myself of them."*

His raises his arms aloft, high above his head, hoping those even higher above him are able to see.

His tattered shirt exposes the flesh beneath the cotton, revealing years' worth of self-inflicted punishment.

Punishment the man believes he must have deserved, for everybody around him clearly did, as the voices in his head told him time and time again.

> *"They consume me, as they have done since my arrival on Earth, when my dear Mother introduced me to the world. How she suffered, so much, my Lord."*

His Mother, no longer by his side, also a victim of a world that only rejected her. Her suffering, in his mind, only further proof of why he must be punished for his mere existence.

"For so long, I was different, Lord.
Everywhere I went, I was so different, but I tried so hard to be one of them, but never was I accepted, never could I be one of them."

The man has tried over and over to understand, to come to terms with what he must have done wrong, aside from simply being born.

His efforts were only ever in vain, constantly rejected despite attempting every method he could learn.

"To make matters worse, there was no role in the nativity of life for me, Lord. Not as the sheep, nor the Shepherd, nor anything or anybody else. How can you exit stage left when you were never even able to enter the stage at all?"

This is something that stings him, the inability to express his faith and worship in an act of charisma in front of an audience.

After all, if he couldn't be accepted in a regular sense, at least, surely, he could've been accepted as part of something, as part of a collective, something that would bring joy to people.

And, of course, by "the people," one means the masses who are only ever satisfied by entertainment, believing themselves to be experiencing a kind of spiritualism through a medium fomented by the kinds of people who spit in the face of true spiritual awakening, directed instead by finance and perversion.

"They never understood me, my Lord, just as they never understood you."

Of course, the Lord who taught the message of peace, but who fell afoul of belonging to a tribe who dance to the sound of the coin.

He, the Lord, who fell afoul of being born amongst the wrong people, teaching a message to those who could never understand, and would only utilise his message and his purpose as a means of turning those unlike them into slaves and cattle.

"From early on, they held me in rooms and performed what they called "analysis." They deemed me to be "mentally ill." They deemed my actions with words cushioned so that I wouldn't be harmed by them, but the people outside of those walls had already harmed me with their words... and their actions."

Yes, the man remembers those rooms so well, with their comfy seats that may as well have been concrete thrones.

Their analysis, their programmes, their support networks... all so pitiful.

They judged the man and his Mother with such cruelty, cruelty not so faintly hidden behind words of "encouragement," until the time came when they could apparently do no more, and they simply tossed the Son and the Mother out to fend for themselves, deeming that the time had come for the son to follow the path all good fools must, to serve the greater good of society and simply figure out how to make it all work. All while ignoring the damage done by those whose crimes they simply did nothing about.

"There was nothing I could do, Lord, to appease or please them. I tried, every day, to be what they wanted me to be, but it only left me switching evermore."

Switching personas, personas whose development would keep the man awake every night, and with so little sleep, how could he possibly function?

"My body fits and contorts at night in the dark, after another day of fighting to keep the freakery away. It's the demons, my Lord, I know it. They work to disfigure me, to humiliate me in front of the world, so I must fight them in the day, when your light gives me strength, but at night, they thrive in the darkness, and that is when they win. I cannot stop them in the dark, trying to do so is too much, my Lord. Forgive me."

And the sleep that he has managed to achieve over the years, filled with nightmares too horrific to describe. The demons he sees, believing them to be those he was warned of in his studies of the holy words, brought about by the horrors of his existence, of his lifelong experiences.

He doesn't realise it, but these demons are those he has encountered throughout his life. He wasn't able to be a part of the nativity, but inside his mind at night, he is part of an entirely different production, one in which he is the "main attraction," where the audience mocks and ridicules him as his "supporting cast" put him through the same horrors he has experienced his entire life over and over again.

He is never free.

It never leaves.

The show goes on and on.

"So cruel, has this life been, that I cannot take anymore. I am so sorry, my Lord, but while I pray that my soul will pass on and fight for eternity, fight for you and everything that you are, my physical self simply cannot stand what Earth forces it to go through day after day."

And here, you begin to realise what his supposed "final sin" truly is.

The sin he has supposedly committed is the conclusion he has come to.

The final sin is what he is about to do. He raises himself from his knees, standing with intent for the first time in his life, eyes to the heavens above, as he calls out these words.

"And so, here I stand, atop a mountain cliff. I stand in your image, my Lord, as Christ the Redeemer, and I beg you for your forgiveness, and I beg you to forgive me for what I am about to do, and I beg that you will be there on the other side. My arms are spread aloft, and my body will fall from the mountain top. I pray, o' Lord, that while my body will succumb, that you will catch my soul and take me away from this pain. Forgive me, Lord, for I know not what I am supposed to have done wrong."

And so, he falls from the mountain top, finding peace in his final moments, and though he doesn't know it, though his physical body will fall and succumb to death, his spirit will indeed be caught, and on the other side he will learn the truth, and once he does, he will finally know true peace.

Number 9, Number 9, Number 9...

It Begins. Again.

I am trapped. No, not simply trapped. I am lost.

Lost in this darkened room, where I have been for so long, with no means of escape.

No matter, I am not alone.

No, I have this little record player with me, keeping me company. Playing just one song.

One song, that isn't even a song.

"Number 9, Number 9, Number 9..."

Loops and swirls, loops and swirls.

I have heard it all before, and yet it sounds so new, despite being decades old.

The horror never ages, however.

Sometimes it sounds like the films of that era. Makes sense, I suppose, unlike the sounds that actually emanate from it.

"Every one of them knew that as time goes by, they'd get a little bit older and a little bit slower."

Loops again, like a clown tooting a horn on LSD, laughing all the while.

"Number 9, Number 9, Number 9..."

A baby coos, like all babies do, not knowing anything of the world around them.

A tiny little hint of innocence in a world of horror.

Make it stop.

"Number 9, Number 9, Number 9..."

But there are more voices, and now... GRANDIOSITY!!

A brass band plays! But there's a howl, like a car siren howling down a motorway tunnel.

Revolution.

A world in motion.

People shout.

People fight.

John... stop shouting!!

Nothing about this is right!

Nothing about this is all right!!

"Number 9, Number 9, Number 9..."

Ding dong, and some elegant voices, but there's beeping, like a toy car that's got the hiccups. And now there's happiness, and a man calling through something.

A car rides off.

A world in motion.

George says something about the situation.

Is that John saying we are standing still?

Is Paul reading the Telegraph?

Why is that man imitating a chimp?!?

"Number 9, Number 9, Number 9..."

Two voices, then a howl.

Then more voices.

Revolution now!

Apocalypse now!

We want it, and we want it now!

The sounds of the Revolution!

R E V O L U T I O N

They know not what they ask for.

"Number 9, Number 9, Number 9..."

TISH, TISH, TISH!!!

Loops and whirls, loops and whirls.

And screams, and a man calling over the top.

Make it stop.

Please.

Make them all stop.

Damn them all!! Damn them all to hell!!

"I am not in the mood..."

Stop laughing, John. None of this is funny. She's turning you into a madman.

WAR!!!

WAR!!!

WAR!!!

"Number 9, Number 9, Number 9..."

"Number 9, Number 9, Number 9..."

Wait, what was it they said about that particular bit when it's played backwards?

"Number 9, Number 9, Number 9..."

Wasn't it...?

"Turn me on, Deadman. Turn me on, Deadman. Turn me on, Deadman."

I feel dead, man.

Elderon? Don't you mean Alderaan? And we all know what happened there...

"Take this brother, may it serve you well"

What are you giving me? Madness? I've already had my fair share of that, to be quite honest with you, but I was always taught to be thankful and what not, y'know what I mean?

Oh.

Oh, that's exotic.

That's almost peaceful.

Peculiar, but peaceful.

It sounds quite nice, until the man starts singing. Leave that to the horror films, will you...

Then again...

Drip, drip, drip.

Why is her voice distant?

Why is a freight train heading straight towards me?

What did Yoko just say?

I'll keep my clothes on, thank you very much!! My mind has already been stripped bare; you're not having the clothes off my back!! I don't care if no one can see me in this darkened room!!

No one can see.

Alone.

But not entirely...

They're shouting again.

Please stop it.

Make it stop.

Wait, what?

"Block that kick!! Block that kick!! Block that kick!!"

When did we get on the gridiron?

How did we get here?

And they say madness isn't fun!

That's because it isn't.

I won't be going anywhere soon.

It'll be starting again in a minute.

"Number 9, Number 9, Number 9..."

The Tragedy of the Ghosts

"Bloody hell, John! Where's this come from? I thought it'd be over by last night but it's only gotten worse!"

Jane tried to manoeuvre her body to allow herself to stretch out some of the soreness in her muscles, but the fatigue wouldn't allow it. Wedged in at the end of the sofa, she had tried constantly to stretch out her legs and arms, but instead found herself just falling limp and almost comatose. The cold she had come down with had started to reveal itself some forty-eight hours earlier on the Thursday night, but while she had followed all the usual measures to combat it, it had only worsened since.

So much for the plans for this weekend...

"Must've been something going around," John, her husband, replied. "I don't understand how we've not been affected by it, to be honest."

"Suzy had to go home early on Wednesday," Jane noted, "and Theresa hadn't been in at all since leaving at lunch on Monday. I wasn't the only one to leave within the first half hour of the shift starting yesterday either. Jim & Ed were both gone earlier than I was."

"Which basically confirms that it was something going around," John replied in deadpan fashion. "Look, the only thing we can do is make sure you do nothing but relax! And I don't want any rejection of that policy, either, you do enough as it is, sweetheart."

"Oh, stop fussing, love," Jane chuckled with a wheeze.

"Don't worry, Dad, we'll make sure she doesn't set foot off that couch!"

Jane and John glanced around to face the direction where the young voice had emanated, where their son, Fred, stood with a mile-wide grin on his face and a brew in either hand.

"Two teas, milky & sugary as ever, correct?" he asked jovially.

"Of course, young sir!" his Father boomed in response, as Fred strolled over and set the cups on the table in front of his parents.

"And don't worry, Mum, a plate of assorted dry biscuits is on the way!" Fred beamed as he turned to his face his Mother. "Perfect for any ill stomach struggling to hold food!"

His parents turned to face each other, the looks on their faces falling somewhere between proud and amused.

"Speaking of which," Fred continued, "your nibbles have arrived!"

And so they had, the plate on which the biscuits sat being carried from the kitchen into the living room by Fred's twin sister, Frances.

"All your favourites are here, Mum!" the young girl said as she reached the sofa. "Guaranteed to fight the fungus currently knocking you for six!"

"'Fight the fungus', have you heard this?" John said to Jane with a chuckle.

"Oh, I have," Jane replied with a chortle of her own. "God, she reminds me so much of Bea..."

"I heard that," Frances interjected, beaming as she did so. "When's she coming to visit? I know she loves Iceland an' all that but *we* love *her* so it'd be nice to see her again. Or maybe we could go and visit her?"

"Listen, in this state, I'll be lucky if I cross the street any time soon," Jane said with a splutter. She took the plate of biscuits from her daughter, snuggling up to her husband as she did as an illness-induced shiver ran through her.

The twins sat themselves down on the smaller sofa that was angled differently from its larger counterpart. Fred and Frances had opted for solidarity with their Mother's plight, they too enjoying a cup of tea and a handful of biscuits each. The girl, however, shared Jane's bafflement at where the aggressive cold had come from. Clearly it had been going around at work, but where exactly do rough bugs like this suddenly sprout from? More to the point...

"How come Mum's the only one who has been hit like this?" Frances asked, genuinely curious, if not a little concerned, as to whether her Mother was more susceptible to succumbing to such bugs as opposed to the rest of the household. "We've not even been touched by it. It's not like we've had mild symptoms at all, we've just not even had a cold of any kind."

"Simple answer to that, dear sister of mine," Fred chirped mischievously, "we're simply made of sturdier stuff in contrast to our frail ol' Mum."

"Oi, less of that!" Jane wheezed back, wagging her finger. "Otherwise, I'll milk this for all it's worth and make sure you and only you are the one doing my bidding, young man."

Sensing an opportunity, Fred replied "One little problem there, Mum. You've basically just admitted you'd be fibbing, and as such none of us would be obliged in any way to adhere to your whims."

Jane was about to retort, until she realised her boy had outwitted her. Twisting her lips, she glanced to face her husband next to her, who simply sat facing forward looking like Dennis the Menace, clearly enjoying the scene of familial banter.

"Cheeky little git," she whispered to John, trying to disguise her own amused smile. "He gets this from you!"

"From me?" John humorously barked in innocence. "Hang about, apparently Fran gets her wordplay from Bea while Fred supposedly gets his wit from me, are there no contributions of your own, dearest wife?"

Refusing to fall into any more of her beloved family's comedic traps, she simply took a sip of tea, rolled her eyes and gazed lovingly at them all, though she insisted on putting her daughter's mind at ease.

"Don't worry, sweetheart," she said, softly. "Some people just get sucker punched by these bugs in different ways. I'll be fine, we all will."

The four of them shared smiles, and settled into their cups of tea, with John comically pinching a couple of Jane's biscuits to make up for the lack of his own, much to the twin's amusement.

It was a quiet, late-September Saturday night, and the Autumn of 1990 was beginning to truly show its face. The nights seemed to fade into darkness sooner and sooner every night, while the green leaves of the summer were entering their twilight, as they aged, browned and crisped. For this family of four, an extremely close-knit unit, nights like this one were nothing particularly special or peculiar. Aside from occasional family catch-ups, they had often made themselves their own company, and it would more than likely continue to be the case. John was an only child born to parents who in turn had no siblings, and so extended family members had simply never been something he had needed to worry about. Jane, on the other hand, was the eldest of three daughters, and had for years been somewhat of a leading light for her younger sisters, Beatrice and Molly. Times had changed in recent years, however. While the three sisters remained inexplicitly close, their age gaps and different life paths had inevitably led them to growing apart somewhat. At 35, Jane was the eldest, having married John relatively early before giving birth to the twins at 22. Beatrice, the stereotypical 'Middle One,' was headstrong and driven to be a part of something she believed herself destined to, although her individuality never outweighed the love she carried for her sisters. Now 28, she had moved to Iceland some five years earlier, having felt heavily drawn there as a result of her ancestry. Molly, meanwhile, was 20 and heavily involved in artistic ventures, ventures that Jane actively encouraged her to utilise to her full potential and make the most of.

The three sisters were charismatic, intelligent and loving, both individually and as a collective, but the fact that they had drifted added further weight to the already fatigued muscles throughout Jane's body. More discrete, yet more damaging, was the impact the stress left on Jane's mind. Beatrice had always been quite blunt about such worries whenever the three sisters discussed them together; "we're all a bit screwed up in this family." But Jane couldn't allow them to show, especially if any judgement could potentially be passed on her which would negatively impact the twins. They had already been through so much, the last thing she could afford was them bearing the burden of their Mother being branded as loopy.

Thinking about what the twins had endured only added even further stress. Jane couldn't be prouder of them, neither could John, nor their Aunties. Molly in particular doted on them, and Jane made a point of ensuring they spent as much time with Molly as possible. Beatrice, too, had been amazing with them prior to her departure. In fact, a special memory they all shared could be seen atop the fireplace. A polaroid photo with "1985" scribbled in the corner, taken during the last true family gathering before Beatrice set off for Iceland. In it were the three sisters, cuddling each other and the twins in front of them. Beatrice had intended to have three such pictures taken so that each sister would be in possession of one, but alas, one had spoilt, and so only she and Jane were able to have a copy.

If only Beatrice could be here to really allow the twins to forget about school every once in a while. Molly's need to focus on her art, as encouraged by Jane, meant she couldn't always be there, and Jane & John's respective work schedules had left them spending less and less time with their children, a factor worsened by the horrendous bullying endured by the twins at school. They had always been eccentric, despite being quite reserved at the same time, but that didn't excuse the ridicule they had endured throughout both primary school and secondary school. Jane occasionally took the time to thank the gods she had had twins as opposed to just one child, as she couldn't bear to think what either Fred or Frances would've been going through had they not had the other alongside them. They were a perfect foil for each other, that much was certain, and even in their darkest moments they gave each other the strength to carry on smiling, though both Jane & John knew this was often done in the hope that it would prevent them from worrying. John kept it to himself, but he often found himself guilt-ridden. Jane, meanwhile, much like Beatrice & Molly, found herself crippled by self-loathing, often blaming herself for her babies' suffering, despite knowing full well she had done everything she could throughout their thirteen years and being constantly reminded, particularly by Molly, that she was an incredible Mother. Indeed, Molly had specifically said that Jane was "meant to be a Mum."

Speaking of Molly...

The home phone sat perched on a little table beside the sofa, conveniently right next to Jane's left arm, and it began to ring. Suddenly cut off from her thoughts, she gave a little jerk, before swinging her head round to where the ringing was coming from, before quickly gathering herself and answering the phone.

"Hello? Mol! How are you? Nevermind me, how are *you*? No, I said nevermind *me*, how are *you*? Some bloody cold isn't going to be my downfall, little sister, despite the witty remarks made by a certain young gentleman earlier."

Fred grinned to himself as he, his sister and his Father all watched Jane as she nattered away to her sister over the phone. It didn't come as any surprise to any of them that Molly had made a point of ringing to check up on Jane. This weekend was supposed to have been so different. The original plan, which for all intents and purposes had still been active as of Thursday lunchtime, would have seen John, Jane and the twins stay with Molly and the twins' grandparents from Friday night right through to Monday morning. The intention was to enjoy a much-needed family gathering in which Jane & Molly could catch-up, Molly would be able to fall right back into her role of doting Auntie, the grandparents would be able to spend time with the twins, and even John would be able to relax in good company. John & Jane had gone so far as to not only each booking Monday off from work, but had even concocted an excuse for the twins to be off school that day, which would have allowed them all to spend the Sunday night with the relatives and then return home at their own leisure on the Monday. The family had almost been able to smell the Sunday roast for weeks, only to have such a delightful sensation cruelly robbed from them by Jane's affliction.

Not all was lost, however, as they had agreed to push the gathering back by a single week, and while they wouldn't be able to stay the Sunday night, they would at least be able to enjoy Friday night, all through Saturday and the majority of Sunday in good company. All they could do now was keep their fingers tightly crossed in the hope that Jane would recover in time. At least she wouldn't be bogged down by work in the meantime, and of course she would be able to be there for the twins before and after school all week, which was very rarely the case.

Always nice to find spots of light amidst the darkness.

"Just make sure Mum keeps Dad to making the gravy. He might burn his dumplings, but no man I know stirs gravy better than our Father!"

Though she was coughing and wheezing, it was good to see Jane laughing and smiling for once. Regardless of the cold, her smiles were too often forced, ironically for the benefit of her family, just as it was often the case for the twins when they were trying to put their parents' minds at ease. Now, however, she was in her element, having a right good chit-chat with her little sister, thinking of better days to come. It was that desire to constantly see, and indeed aim for and work towards, a better future which probably drove the family forward. For all their troubles and struggles, they just somehow believed that they could achieve a better life. Fred & Frances constantly talked about the things they wished to do, believing it was their duty to ensure their parents could rest in the years to come, while both of them excitedly predicted that they would take pride in their future cousins looking up to them. Molly had already told them she intended to give any potential daughter of hers the name 'Sally,' which in turn had left the twins attempting to metaphorically paint a vision of the future. John & Jane meanwhile saw their sole combined purpose in life as one that would give their twins the platform needed to best avoid any and all barriers to a prosperous life. This was a family that not only loved each other, but believed in each other & saw in each other the road to a better future together.

"Mol, don't worry about it. I'll be all clear in a few days at worst, and then next weekend we'll be able to make up for it. Just give Mum & Dad our love, tell 'em we can't wait to come round."

The phone call soon came to an end with the usual loving pleasantries and goodbyes, before Jane put the phone down and informed John and the twins that Molly was thinking about them all.

"We haven't seen Auntie Mol enough recently," Frances said, longingly. "She had an idea for us where she wanted us to try and do some paintings with her. She challenged us to come up with scenes based around our books and records. We'll have to make sure we get around to it next weekend."

"She'll make an amazing Mother herself, one day," Jane said in response. "I just wish she'd stop worrying so much about everything, she's still only young, it'll bloody cripple her at this rate."

"To be honest, love," John interjected, "I think it'll do you both the world of good to spend time with each other again."

"You won't get an argument out of me there," Jane smiled. "By the way, did we lock the front door earlier?"

"I think so," John answered. "Don't worry about it, it'll be fine. It'll be locked before we go to bed, anyway."

The evening thus carried on as normal. The twins made a point of making fresh brews once their mugs had been emptied, while their parents were engaged in conversation regarding some long-term work and finance matters. The twins themselves were also engaged in conversation, as was often the case. Usually, they were discussing books and records, hence Molly's challenge to them to each create a piece of art inspired by those great loves of theirs. This evening was no different, as they found themselves discussing the nuances of Nirvana's *Bleach* album that had been released the year before. Once again, it was Molly's influence that had triggered this discussion, as she was a considerably enthusiastic fan of the relatively new band from Aberdeen, Washington. The album in question was something the twins had been able to have a listen to when they last saw their Auntie, and it hadn't really been like anything they'd heard before. Sure, hard rock was at its foundation, and its influences were identifiable to some degree, but it also seemed to carry some other intriguing features, such as the singer's vocals & riffs and the basslines were proper, well, grungy. The twins had kept an eye out for a follow-up, but while Molly had told them she had read reports of a second album being in production, there were no signs of it in the music shops yet.

Nevermind, all in good time...

As the twins returned from the kitchen, both carrying a mug of tea in each hand, Fred seemed to stop in his tracks just as he placed his Dad's brew down on the table.

"You alright, son?" John asked him, noticing the youngster's sudden pause as he had begun to straighten himself.

Once upright, Fred pulled a face and looked towards the living room window. He paused momentarily, before answering.

"I thought I heard something outside. Not sure what, but it just sounded like... I don't know. Sorry."

"No need to apologise, kidder," John replied. "It'll be nothing, probably just one of the neighbours doing a bin run. Thanks for the brew."

"Same here," Jane piped up, before sipping from the mug Frances had passed to her.

"Our pleasure as ever," the daughter replied as she sat down before setting her own mug on the table. "Fred, it's nothing, don't worry about it."

Her brother clearly wasn't convinced, as he had made his way towards the window. The curtains were drawn, and Fred still had his own cup of tea in his hands, so he discretely freed his left hand to gently create a gap between the curtains to allow him to peep through the window.

"I just want to have a lo-... hang on! Who's this?!?"

None of the others in the room had time to ask "Who's who?" or "Who's what?" before they heard the front door opening. Before they knew it, a scruffy, shaven headed man stood in their living room, having kicked the front door shut behind him.

John was the first to react, immediately getting to his feet and about to unload a verbal barrage on the man until the latter revealed a gun in his possession, which he quickly pointed directly at John.

"Not so fast, superstar," the intruder obnoxiously taunted. "Sit yourself back down."

John didn't immediately acquiesce, but Jane made a point of tugging at the tail-end of his shirt as a means of encouraging him to sit.

"Just do as he says," she mumbled, a newfound fear evident in her voice. It was a fear that not only found itself rushing through Jane, but in turn stung John. His family were suddenly under severe threat, and he had to just sit there! To make matters even worse, Frances looked utterly terrified, while Fred stood frozen by the window, trying to be brave but instead his petrified gaze just burning a hole into the intruder.

"You wanna lock your bloody doors, any ol' somebody could just come barging in," the intruder barked mockingly. "In fact, you wanna teach your kids some manners!"

"Now listen-" John began to say, until the intruder again strengthened the emphasis in which he pointed the gun, before interrupting.

"Nah, I think you'll listen to me! A few days ago, these two young brats of yours got into a little argument at school with my young cousin, Vic. Clearly not knowing there are some lines in life you don't cross, they made a point of highlighting my troubles with the law in front of everybody around them. How they happened to find out about my troubles is another matter, but my young cousin keeps to himself. He's a bit brash sometimes, a bit ridiculous, but he keeps to himself. What he doesn't need is young turds inadvertently making his life a misery."

The family glanced around at each other, clearly exasperated. Whatever the twins had done at school was clearly up for debate, but how to respond to this particular situation was another matter altogether. One that required cool heads for starters...

"Alright," John began, "I clearly need to have a word with my kids. But a stupid spat at school doesn't excuse you holding my family at gun point!"

"Well, I tend to disagree," the intruder replied, stepping forward ever so slightly. In doing so, Frances lost control of herself for a moment, quickly dashing up from the smaller sofa and rushing over to the fireplace. She would've preferred to be hiding behind her parents, but she just needed to get away from this fiend. Speaking of which, he began to laugh with heinous delight at her plight, a crude, loud laugh that sounded like it emanated from the dregs of the worst council estate you could imagine. But this fiend, despite his appearance and his apparent taste for crime, didn't appear to be a delinquent. Not intellectually anyway, even if socially he certainly fell into that bracket. He glanced over to Fred, whose gaze was now firmly fixed on his twin sister, a protective sense of fear clearly visible. The fiend coughed to get his attention, and then, using the gun, gestured that he join her by the fireplace. After standing frozen for a second or so, Fred quickly dashed to join Frances, the cup of tea still in his hands spilling over as he did. The flurry of air whipped up by the twins' movements had caused the polaroid atop the fireplace to firstly tip over and secondly fall off entirely, before descending to the floor.

The intruder noticed the fallen picture, and demanded that Fred pick it up and place it on the table so he could see it. As the intruder went to pick it up, Jane felt John nudge slightly as though intending to make another go for the man, but again she tugged him back, god forbid he find himself on the end of a gunshot.

The intruder, having picked up the polaroid with his free hand, took the time to look at it. Fred's tea had spilt on it a little, but the picture itself remained untarnished. At least, it did, until the intruder suddenly pulled a disgusted face and proceeded to tear it in half, before dumping it in Frances' abandoned brew on the table.

"Family," he muttered to himself, before looking back at his terrified hosts. "I bet you all wish your family were here now. Well tough sh-"

"Please can you just go!"

This time it was Jane's turn to blurt out, and doing so caused tears in her eyes to erupt.

"Please, don't hurt my babies! If you want money, I'll give you money, but just take it and go!"

For a moment, the intruder was taken aback, and he appeared to almost sympathise with Jane's distress. Typically, it must've been caused by surprise, as he quickly began laughing at the situation.

"Ha! I didn't actually come for cash but I'll take it anyway!"

John couldn't restrain himself anymore.

"Then why, you sick freak, *are* you here?!?"

The intruder sighed, and had the audacity to perch himself on the arm on the smaller sofa.

"Vic told me on Tuesday night about your brats making him look like an idiot, and in his haste, he asked me to pass by and do some damage to your car or your house or what have you. The following day he rang me telling me not to bother, and I agreed. But you see, something pissed me off. He sounded defeated, like a wounded animal who just wanted to be left alone. And that's something I've seen too often from members of my family. People who found themselves ground down by everybody around and just accepted it, just allowed themselves to be walked over. So, I decided I'd do things differently. I've paid multiple people back over the years for the crap they've put me through, why would I not do the same when my cousin was made to look like a complete prat in front of countless people he already hates?"

"For god's sake, this is ludicrous!" John bit back. "These are just kids. My kids have been through bleeding hell and back in school for years, I've never resorted to this!"

The intruder glared at John, his eyes appearing to swim in hateful waters, and yet his expression also appeared almost blank.

With another sigh, he eventually replied "Pft, pathetic. You'll never understand, people like you."

He stood again, strengthening his grip on his gun again.

As he did, the twins suddenly sprung their hands up in reactive fear, Fred finally dropping his brew as he did.

It hit the edge of the table, and shattered as the contents spilt onto the carpet. An old mug that belonged to John's grandfather, a tiny little piece of family treasure, gone just like that.

The intruder found himself further irritated, both by the twins' sudden show of fear, as well as the noise and mess made by the destroyed cup of tea.

"Jesus Christ," he muttered to himself. Gesturing to John & Jane with his gun, he said "Right, get up, stand there with your brats, arms in the pissing air! Where are your wallets? I might as well get as much as I can..."

The parents slowly rose from the larger sofa, Jane requiring a bit of support from John in her weak state, and they stood by the fireplace, silently nodding to their children, hoping to be able to provide some kind of support and reassurance.

Once they were in place, John directed the intruder to a small cabinet by the doorway to the kitchen, where his & Jane's wallets could be found.

The intruder didn't bother looking at what was inside, he simply stashed them in his pockets, muttering to himself as he did.

"A bonus is a bonus," he said a little louder as he turned to face the family again. He momentarily seemed to feed off of their fear, and gloated as they did, before apparently deciding he'd done enough, as he turned on his heel and made for the front door.

"You'll pay for this!"

Just as the intruder's hand was about to reach the door handle, he froze, and slowly turned to face the family again. The voice had been weak and fearful, but loud enough and with enough spite to get his attention.

It was Frances. She who had shown the most fear out of all four of them, who stood in the middle between her Mother and her brother, arms weakly raised but with a scowl across her face.

"Sorry, what?" the intruder responded.

A look of horror grew on the faces of her family, but Frances didn't notice them.

"You heard me; you'll pay for this. I just know it. Whether it's us or somebody else, you'll get what you deserve."

The intruder's jaw dipped ever so slightly, and he stood looking rather gormless for a moment.

His head suddenly shifted between family members, as he tried to fathom how to react, but instead he just blurted out a confused laugh, and turned again back to the door.

But again, he froze before he could open it. And again, he began to laugh. No, not a laugh this time. A cackle. He cackled maniacally, and sadistically. To think that Jane and her sisters had been so insecure about talking about their mental state for so many years, and yet here stood a genuine psychopath in their living room, having just well and truly buggered their Saturday night when they shouldn't even have been here.

Once more, he turned to face the family, but this time he focused only on the twins, an evil smile leering across his face.

"You cheeky little shits, you haven't learned at all, have you? You should've kept your little mouths shut."

And with that, his arm was raised, the gun in his hand was pointed, and two shots were fired. One for each twin, squarely in each chest.

The scene erupted into hysteria.

The intruder was gone in an instant, away into the night, his evil deed committed, his fate sealed.

John & Jane utterly capitulated, as their babies collapsed before them. The tea stain left on the carpet by Fred's fallen mug was consumed by a tsunami of red, as the twins' bodies each fell rapidly into a lifeless state. Their parents cried and howled, and as their neighbours from all over the street, alarmed by the gunshots, swarmed in to rush to their aid, all sense of normality & structure completely disintegrated.

The ambulance, called to the home by one of the neighbours, was never going to reach them in time. Various neighbours did everything they could to provide immediate emotional support to the parents, as they would continue to do in the days ahead, but there was nothing that could truly be done for them. Nor for the twins, who's now almost ghostly pale features haunted the minds of all who saw them. These innocent youngsters, with so much to give, had their lives ripped away from them, and nobody who saw them as they passed away would ever be able to escape the heartbreak that they experienced that day. Each of them would have those cold, cruel images burned into their minds for good, just as the cries and howls from John & Jane would haunt their dreams for their remaining days.

***

A numbness gripped them, though they felt horrific agony. The numbness, maybe, was helping to cushion the pain, but at what cost? Pain is to be experienced and learnt from. However, when one suffers pain to such a degree that one loses a grip on reality and begins to feel nothing but numbness, then one effectively ceases to be human, ceases to live.

Ceases to live...

All around them was lost. They could sense great angst, pain and suffering, but the cries and howls seemed to descend into echoes, slowly but surely drifting away.

Despite the numbness taking hold more and more as time passed, the pain remained. The physical pain seemed to last forever, until physicality became a thing of the past, and the physical pain subsided and was succeeded by something far worse, something more brutal, yet unseeable.

Emotional pain.

Devastation, heartbreak, loss.

What surrounded them could not be defined. It was like nothing that had ever been seen before, a hypnotic, adrenalin rush-inducing mania, full of colour and sound, and in a way, they felt as if they were falling despite also remaining completely still. They felt almost weightless, and yet heavier than they had ever felt before.

Maybe the weightlessness was brought about by the abandonment of physicality.

Maybe the newfound weight was the emotional trauma being inflicted upon them.

Feeling an urge to find a sense of understanding, even the slightest hint of normality, the girl tried to call to her brother.

"Fred," she echoed, her voice barely a whisper and yet a cry that filled the void of wherever they were.

"Frances," her brother called back, his own confusion and trauma evident.

Their bodies... no, their spirits, appeared to swing and drift around this place, until they found themselves almost hanging, as though sky diving, their arms stretched out. They found themselves facing one another, fear, terror and heartbreak apparent in their eyes. In desperation, they both reached for one another, hands desperately trying to bring them together, hands that finally met and clasped together, and once they did, everything fell into darkness and silence.

An eternity seemed to pass until they awoke once more. The awakening itself seemed to take far too long, but eventually they came to, and the first thing each of them saw was the other.

They appeared ghostly, and incorporeal. They tried to speak, but no sounds emanated from them. They tried to move, but were barely able to float around. Eventually, when it seemed like one of them was in danger of drifting away, the other would take hold of them just in the nick of time. They didn't know where they were, but they had each other, just as they had always had each other.

Little by little, the things they knew and loved came to them again, like books and records.

The things that they had turned to when the world constantly rejected them.

They remembered those films they loved so much... Star Wars! They loved Star Wars!

And the music... that record they spoke of, the Nirvana record! A sense of excitement grew between them, and it gave them new life with each passing moment. Then, as their identities seemed to rebuild, they remembered their most beloved; their parents!

"Where are they?" the girl blurted out, surprising herself as she did, these being the first words of her new self.

"I don't know," the boy replied, uttering his own first new words. "Let's find them!"

And so, that's what they attempted to do. It seemed to take another age, but they tried to drift around this peculiar realm they found themselves in. It was all white, like something found in a vision of the future, though they soon realised they were searching for a specter of the past.

Occasionally, they would call out for their parents, but no reply came. The white realm around them seemed to be able to speak to them, but though they silently asked for something that revealed the presence of their parents, no sufficient answer was given.

They weren't there.

They couldn't be found.

"Where are they?" the girl asked once more.

"I don't know," the boy replied once more, but this time he made no suggestion of trying to find them. Though he didn't say as such, he knew they were gone, and so did she.

But then something more seemed to come to him, a new sense of realisation, albeit one that haunted him as the truth began to grow and reveal itself.

Their appearances were developing, and they began to more closely resemble who they were, or maybe, who they are. But with that development came the looks that they carried when their emotions began to show. And the boy's fear was showing.

"What's wrong?" the girl asked, her concern obvious.

He took a moment to reply, but when he did, he asked "We're siblings, aren't we?"

The girl, too, took a moment to reply to his question, but eventually she nodded and answered "Yes. Yes, we are."

"But... who are we?"

That question, however, was one the girl couldn't answer. She tried to, immediately believing she could utter her own name and that of her brother, and any confusion would be cleared away. But she couldn't, and she found herself scared as a result. How was this possible? They knew what they liked, they knew their parents, they knew each other, but not *who* they were. More time seemed to pass as they were almost frozen watching each other, trying to figure out the truth, until it eventually came to them. *It* came to them. And when *it* came to them, so much of who they were came to them, and so did the cruel truth.

They had been twins, belonging to loving parents, with loving relatives, living in a world that constantly put them down. But they had been there for each other, as they had been throughout this seeming eternity in this realm. But they had been...

They had been murdered.

That fiend.

He was the cousin of the one from school, Vic.

And he had entered their home, taunting their family, before eventually...

Murdering them.

And then more realisation hit them.

In light of the trauma they had experienced, in light of this journey they had taken, the pain and suffering they had gone through had robbed them of their identities. For the most part they had their memories, and thankfully they had each other, but their identities had been stripped away, torn from them just as their lives had been torn from them. Just as their bond with their parents had been torn from them.

With this realisation, they noticed something. The white realm around them appeared to collapse, peculiar cracks appearing all around it before it simply began to disintegrate, and once it did, they began to see the world around them.

And it was a world they recognised.

The garden. They were in the garden. They were home!

Their parents! Would they be here?!? Had they escaped the realm as a result of knowing the truth? Maybe now they could go home!!

The euphoric possibility of reunion lasted mere moments, until the twins glanced at each other and realised the truth. They stretched out with their feelings, but their parents weren't here. They had returned to the home they had always known, but it was no longer the home of their parents.

They were gone.

Pain burned the essences of their spirits, but they found strength in each other, and took the time to gaze at their home.

So many memories, and yet still their identities were a thing of the past. They realised that they were sat in the middle of their garden, legs crossed, sat next to each as they often had when they were younger.

"How long has it been, sister?" the brother asked, his gaze remaining fixated on the home.

This time it was her turn to reply. "I don't know. But I think our home belongs to somebody else now."

The brother looked harder, and noticed somebody in the kitchen. It was a lady, but it wasn't his Mother. She had brown hair that fell to her shoulders, whereas his Mother's hair fell further down her back to her shoulder blades. This lady's face was tired, yet also warm whilst also appearing to be one of strength. His Mother's face was also warm and tired, but was also one that silently expressed gentle leadership as opposed to cracking the whip where necessary.

He noticed the lady turn to look over her shoulder.

"George," she called out, "are you coming helping me with these pots?"

A few seconds passed, and the twins watched with intrigue, as a young boy of maybe ten years of age appeared by her side.

"You go and sit down, Mum," he said when he reached her. "I'll do these, and I'll make you and Dad a brew each when I'm done."

"Are you sure?" the boy's Mother asked him, resting a hand on his shoulder.

"Course," the boy replied. "Go on, I'll be back in shortly."

The lady smiled, wrapped an arm around his shoulders with a tight squeeze, and left him to do his chore. He washed the pots as he said he would, occasionally glancing out of the window as he did. The twins wondered whether he could see them, but it quickly became apparent to them that he couldn't, which could surely mean only one thing.

They were ghosts.

The very thought momentarily filled them with horror, though it was a horror that subsided as they glanced at each other, and then back at the boy. Though only young, the boy's demeanour seemed to be one of somebody with the world on his shoulders. He would occasionally scowl to himself, as though something was bothering him, or indeed multiple things were bothering him. The twins, almost immediately, felt a sense of similarity with this boy. They also pondered the white realm they had seemingly left behind, and how it had seemed to speak to them. Was it the new presence emanating from their home, calling to them?

An abundance of questions flushed over them, but as they glanced at each other once more, they shared a little smile, as though a new sense of realisation had dawned on them, this time one with far more of a positive theme.

Though they had no concept of the passage of time, it seemed to them that a number of weeks were passing by as they watched this family that now occupied their home. There were three of them; a Father, a Mother and the son, George. Much like their own family, they seemed to be extremely close-knit and very eccentric, although sadly the time they spent together appeared to be limited. They noticed that the boy spent a lot of time on his own both before and after school, as his parents seemed to work long, harsh hours much like their own had done. Occasionally they would be able to eavesdrop on conversations, as they learnt vaguely of the boy's struggles at school and the parents' desires to provide for their collective family unit whilst looking out for each other and providing constant emotional support. They also briefly heard the Mother encouraging George to speak to a girl from his class, though the boy had appeared to quickly knock that particular topic on the head before it could develop.

What quickly became apparent to the twins, though how they discovered this they didn't truly understand, was that they had returned for good reason. Their spirits were intricately bonded with this home, not simply because it had been theirs but also because of the trauma of their deaths. They had found a family similar to their own, and they quickly believed that they had a new purpose. This family was suffering, and the darkness that latched itself onto the home as a result of the events of the past threatened to do irreparable damage to them, and that was something the twins simply couldn't allow. They quickly realised that they could fight the darkness that threatened to consume this family, and as a result could indirectly shift the family's fortunes in a more favourable direction. How all of this was possible was, frankly, beyond the twins' knowledge, but they cared not. They had a purpose, and they were determined to fulfill it.

As the weeks passed, the boy had seemingly begun his final year of primary school, and his first few weeks in this final year were already having a damaging effect. It was also around this time that something dawned on the twins; they were not here simply to keep the darkness at bay, nor simply to quietly aid the family. They were here to forge a pathway for both George and his family, and also themselves. What that pathway would entail, and what it would lead to, they weren't entirely sure, especially as they foresaw large swathes of unpreventable darkness from afflicting the family in the future despite their best efforts. Regardless, something told them that they needed to directly intervene with the family as a means of triggering a chain of events that would bring George and his family in line with a better future, much as they themselves had hoped for their own family, whilst in turn setting them on the road to what they desired; the realisation of who they were... no, who they *are,* and the peace they could finally enjoy!

They would need to tread cautiously, and they would need to trigger a sense of inspiration within the young boy as opposed to directing every little decision he would take, but they knew what they had to do.

One Autumn afternoon, George had returned home from school, looking as desperate as he had for weeks, when the twins were gathering the strength they needed. He had glanced out of the kitchen window, appearing to notice something different about the breeze blowing about his garden, but he had shrugged it off as nothing. The twins saw this as a positive sign for the hours ahead, and as the darkness eventually fell over the neighbourhood, and the family prepared to drift off to sleep for the night, they were ready.

Ready to reveal themselves, ready to initiate their purpose, ready to make a difference and ready to begin this new journey.

It was time.

Time for a damaged young soul to be guided by the ghosts...

The Man Who Never Returned

Sunday night arrived with little issue, as two men in tailored suits sat opposite one another in the corner of the local public house as planned. The first man had arrived some twenty minutes or so earlier, while the second man had followed him about fifteen minutes later. Having rested their long jackets and bowler hats on their chairs, the two men were at relative ease, fully intending to adhere to a most distressing matter at hand, a distress only cushioned by the food and beverages available to them. The first man wore a thin moustache and a receding hairline, though he was a relatively cheerful soul with a smile that always put people at ease. His tiredness and fatigue were showing, however, as though the emotional weight of recent events were beginning to take their toll. The second man bore faded sideburns with a full head of hair atop his dome, and he too was viewed as a kind hearted gentleman, though also a man of ambition, albeit conscious of remaining within his moral boundaries. Though his features were not showing the wear and tear visible upon those of his friend, he was certainly carrying additional emotional baggage, fearing that this meeting would almost certainly bring him news he didn't believe he was ready to hear. Thankfully, at least, the public house in general was quiet, with only a small number of regulars in for the night, and the atmosphere in the room mostly dictated to by the crackling and warmth of the large fire beaming out of the middle of the largest wall in the vicinity, as opposed to rapturous voices and clanging glasses, as was probably the case twenty-four hours earlier.

"How've you been, my friend?" the second man asked warmly as he and the other settled in.

"As well as one can hope, I suppose," came the first man's response. "Work is work, as you well know. Monotonous for the most part, with the occasional injection of intrigue and fresh development. Occasionally, one finds that a new challenge can make paperwork appear almost exhilarating, until of course everything settles down and monotony reigns supreme once more. How about yourself?"

A smile grew on the second man's face in humour at his friend's reply, as he said "Work is, as you say, work, typically enough. We, too, occasionally find ourselves at risk of discovering new possibilities, until calm returns and we realise another week of our lives has come and gone, with very little changing in the meantime."

"These are the lives we live, good sir," the first man chuckled tiredly, as he turned to face the bar and called for a bottle of brandy and two glasses to be delivered to the table. Upon turning back to face his friend, he asked "Will you be eating?"

"I'm not so sure," the other responded with a shake of the head. "No doubt she-who-must-be-obeyed will have something phenomenal waiting back home later, though she's aware we're having this little meet-up. How, may I ask, is your good lady doing?"

With another weak smile, the first man replied "Cracking the whip as she always does, though, of course, she does so with that sweet smile across her face, reminding me of the love we so deeply share whilst simultaneously letting me knowing that her conviction is well and truly unbreakable."

The two men shared a laugh, and as their brandy and glasses were delivered to their table, they poured themselves a short each, gently clanked their glasses and each took a small sip.

An unspoken inconvenience could not remain unspoken for long, however.

"I fear," the first man began, "that we are avoiding the real reason we meet here, tonight."

Swallowing a hard gulp, the second man failed to hide a hint of fear that spread briefly across his face, before he took a quick breath and prepared himself for the worst.

"I fear you are right," he said. "And so, I must ask, has there been any news?"

Letting out a weary sigh before taking a second sip, the first man eventually answered "The good news and the bad news is simply 'No.' There is no sight nor sound of him. It is as it was when we last met. It's like he has simply vanished off of the face of the Earth, or even ceased to exist."

The second man's face remained, to his relief, neutral.

"The good news being that at least he hasn't turned up dead, or that word has not yet been received of his death," he said. "The bad news being that we still know nothing of his whereabouts."

"Correct," the first man answered simply.

The two men sat in silence for a few minutes, preferring to consume their drinks as opposed to stirring over small nothings. There was no update, and thus there was nothing to discuss. Though, of course, that wasn't entirely true.

The man in question that they spoke of was a good friend to both of them. An eccentric, a creator, a visionary and indeed lauded by some as a genius. His presence amongst his friends had often caused frustration, almost simply as a result of his wild imagination and ambition which often his friends simply could not keep up with or even simply understand. Even the ambition of the second man at the table in this public house paled in comparison to that of the missing friend. In addition to his eccentric nature and his pure genius, he was quite simply a great man in every sense of the word. Respectful, humble, comedic, yet simultaneously, despite his colourful persona, he was also quite reserved and introverted in his own way. More important, however, particularly to the man himself, was his role as Husband and Father. It was his pride in these roles that only added further intrigue, confusion and indeed worry to the matter of his disappearance.

The man had been known to have many elaborate ideas and plans he wished to enact as a means of adhering to his ambitions, at times almost a slave to his need to quench his thirst for breaking new ground. Prior to his marriage, it wasn't uncommon for the man to go missing for days or even weeks upon end. Having lost his only remaining family by his early twenties, the man felt no need to restrain himself when it came to his dreams, and so was known to dive head first into them at every opportunity. His disappearances would cause concern amongst his friends, but the more common they became, the more they came to trust his judgement and know full well that he would return, which he always did.

His marriage, however, had brought to an end his days of extended absence. His friends found relief in this, more out of a sense of thankfulness that they no longer needed to worry that someday he may never return. Additionally, they also found comfort in the fact that the man's marriage didn't fall into the category so often seen when ambitious men acquiesce to marriage. That category, of course, is the one that many men, and indeed women, find themselves in when their new spouse looks upon their dreams with sour eyes and thus brings them to a halt. Instead, the man's friends found peace knowing that the lady he had fallen in love with in fact shared his ambitions and enthusiasm, and that it was in fact *his* desire to dedicate himself to her and the future they intended to share that had brought his days of adventure to a sudden conclusion.

Just the fact that he had eventually become a married man had come as a surprise to his friends. They had quietly been certain that he would never allow himself to open up to the possibilities of love and companionship, instead believing he would chain himself to his dreams forever. When the lady in question originally came along, she and the man had seemed like polar opposites in some ways, and yet they quickly developed a bond rarely seen. Hannah was her name, and she too had benefitted in many ways from the relationship just as he had. They had seemed to bring each other to a new way of thinking and living, and so had improved each other in the process. It took just nine months following their marriage for their daughter, Rose, to arrive. They were, or hopefully 'still are' as the man's friends clung onto, a beautiful family.

"I have to ask," the second man eventually said, breaking the silence in the process, "how is Hannah?"

The first man instantly looked sullen, clearly wishing he could drown himself in the depths of his glass, which he distressingly found to be empty.

"Alas, my friend, not good," he replied.

Picking up the bottle of brandy, he liberally refilled his glass, clearly hoping to make this one last a little longer whilst intending to feel more of an impact from it. Once satisfied with the amount in his glass, he took another, more aggressive swig, and continued.

"Not good at all. She tries to hold strong, god bless her, but you can see she is breaking. I prefer to keep my distance out of respect, but whenever our paths have crossed, she appears to have edged ever closer to the abyss, her eyes looking more and more lost each time. If it were not for the presence of Rose, then I would fear for Hannah's fate with utter dread. The young girl is every inch her Father's Daughter, with her striking blue eyes and elegant brown hair. She is such a symbol of innocence, but you can begin to see the confusion in her at the disappearance of her Father. I fear that at some point she will simply forget who he ever was, though I've no doubt Hannah will do everything she can to ensure young Rose will never forget her Father."

The second man sat in silence for a moment, watching his friend, before he too refilled his glass with brandy, albeit somewhat more conservatively than his counterpart had moments earlier. He too, however, took a rather aggressive swig once his glass had been topped up, clearly also desiring to feel the punch it packed.

"Forgive me for saying this, my friend," he began, "but those latter words sound like those of a man who is beginning to lose faith."

His comments, though without malice, stung the other man, who felt an instant dose of shame which was apparent on his face, which in turn left a feeling of guilt running through the man facing him.

The first man ran his hands over his balding head, holding them in place for a few seconds, before looking up again to face his friend.

"I cannot tell a lie," he whispered, "I fear the worst. And yes, I feel shame as a result."

The second man shook his head, replying "Feel no shame at all. We're all worried to our core that we may have seen him for the last time. The question remains, however; why? Why has he departed again after at least a five-year gap? What could possibly have driven him to leave, especially now he has Hannah & Rose? Was there any indication he was planning this?"

"From what I gather," the first man sighed, "he and Hannah have casually discussed different plans and ideas for some time. The most prominent idea was one that centered around moving away to the coast, raising Rose in a more idyllic environment, and he had spoken at length of visiting different possible destinations to aid their final decision."

"So, we know that he's at least had the idea of taking trips away for a very specific reason, then," the other man replied. "There's no scientific or experimental purpose behind a journey such as that, but that still doesn't explain why he hasn't returned. After all, if he was staying somewhere, even if only temporarily, he could easily make contact with us."

"Exactly," the first man said. "However, it becomes more complicated than that."

"What do you mean?" his friend asked him.

The first man paused before he responded, favouring another sip of his brandy as his bottom lip curled somewhat as wave after wave of thoughts crashed around his head. He had tried to prepare himself for this next bit, as it seemed to dip somewhere into the realms of the unbelievable, and he feared either not doing the topic any justice or his friend simply dismissing the matter out of hand.

"Hannah managed to share some additional information the last time we spoke," he finally managed to say. "She, too, struggled to understand exactly what was going through his head, but from what she could make out, she believes that he was fixated not only with the idea of moving away to somewhere quieter, but also with the possibility of 'making things better.' He had been scribbling notes for months, doodling diagrams of god knows what, things she couldn't understand whenever she was able to look at them. He would often insist all was well, often drip-feeding hints of what he had in mind. It has led to the creation of a fresh fear in her mind."

"Make things better?" the second man blurted out, a look of bafflement across his face. "What on Earth does that mean?"

"Again, I don't know," the first man answered tiredly. "Hannah's fear is that he had some grandiose idea in his head that nobody else could possibly understand and that he has tried to implement a plan based on that idea and as a result he has found himself in a sort of trouble we don't even know about."

"Dear god," the second man muttered absently. After a moment of staring into space, he asked "Has Hannah said anything about what he may have said or done the last time she saw him?"

"Yes," the first man replied. "He'd said he was setting off for a walk, but had been particularly loving with his family that morning. Prior to him walking out through the front door, Hannah had told him not to be too long, but he hadn't properly answered her. He had simply turned to face her, his face in an almost trance-like state, and said 'Worry not. Just remember, there are things to be done of major importance, and we cannot live the lives we wish to without these things being done. More importantly, never forget how much I love you.' I think those words have been haunting her dreams for weeks."

The second man, too, appeared haunted by what he was hearing, as though a world of hypothetical, and indeed haunting, possibilities were engulfing his thoughts.

"Good god, old friend, what have you done?" he asked out loud, as though talking directly to the missing man.

"So yes," the first man said, interrupting the other's pattern of thought, "I fear the worst. I fear that he has been planning something beyond even our collective intellect, and as such has found himself entrapped in something we could never understand. I fear that, he may even have simply gotten himself entangled in some silly misdemeanour, and may be lost or suffering great harm. Most of all, I fear that we may never see him again."

For the third time, the first man refilled his glass with brandy and did his friend the honour of refilling his as well. Words not necessary, the two men quickly clanked their glasses together and downed the contents, ignoring the immediate consequences.

"My friend, I am sorry, but I can be here no longer," the first man said. "I hate the idea of trying to block out his existence, but until I know more, not knowing his fate is killing me, as it is all of us. I must be with my wife, and I advise you do the same."

The second man nodded vigorously; his eyes almost gripped by fear of the unknown. "Yes," he replied sharply. "Yes, you are right. I'm sure we will continue to be held hostage to fear and guilt, but there is nothing we can do, is there..."

"Not for the moment," the other responded. "As ever, if I hear anything, I will contact you. I pray that our friend will join us again at this table as he has done so often in the past, and I will happily accept any mockery of our fear he may wish to throw in our direction, if only so I can shake his hand once more and know he is safe. Not only for his sake, but also for Hannah and Rose."

He stood, and instantly draped himself in his long jacket and placed his hat atop his head. He paused for a moment, which allowed the other man to speak.

"Do you think," the second man began, "that if he doesn't return, we should attempt to seek him out?"

"The thought has crossed my mind," the first man answered. "However, and I cannot properly explain this, so forgive me, something tells me that that duty does not belong to us. I cannot help but believe that, should he be gone for a significant length of time, that duty shall fall to Rose. I'll repeat what I said earlier, she is truly her Father's Daughter. Maybe he knows that himself. Maybe whatever he has done can only be understood by her, and so only she can find him."

"Maybe so," the second man whispered, before dragging himself up from the table and also draping himself in his long jacket and placing his hat atop his head. The two men gave their thanks and acknowledgements to the bartenders, who returned their waves, before they turned to make their way out of the public house.

As they stepped through the old doors, the two of them were embraced by a flush, cold air that rippled through them both. They both looked up to the stars above, gazing almost absently at the scene of many great mysteries that would remain unsolved for generations to come, possibly for eternity in the event that humanity fails to save itself or even simply pull its collective head from its rear.

Many great mysteries...

And here they were, outside in the darkness, consumed by the cold air, just as the truth regarding their friend was lost in the darkness and their hopes were consumed by fear. The two men looked to one another, sharing sad smiles and gentle nods.

"Take care, as always, my friend," the second man said.

"And you, good sir," said the other, as his friend took one last look at the stars and turned to make his way home.

The first man, suddenly alone, also glanced back to the stars. The sadness in his face was exposed by the beams of starlight, and though he paused for a moment, he too eventually turned, albeit in the opposite direction, as he made his way home. As he did, he thought he could hear that beloved song playing somewhere nearby.

How apt, he thought as he walked on by. *One can only hope, old friend...*

We'll meet again
Don't know where, don't know when
But I know we'll meet again
Some sunny day...

Lost On The Hyperlane

"I KNEW WE SHOULD'VE STAYED ON VUSTE!!"

This wasn't happening. This was just *not* happening!

Given everything that had happened over the past few weeks, let alone in the years gone by, this was not the way they were about to meet their end!

Nate & Mallok had travelled from one end of the galaxy to the other more times than they could remember, and never at any point had such a simple voyage gone so wrong. Nate, the Human, was the pilot, with Mallok, the Deesher, his long-time compadre and co-pilot. They had seen worlds of all kinds, faced down foes of various species and survived encounters that would make even the grimmest of the galaxy crawl under a rock. But never had they botched a simple hyperdrive calculation!

"NATE, I DON'T UNDERSTAND! WE HAVEN'T DONE ANYTHING ANY DIFFE-"

The ship swung for the umpteenth time, cutting Mallok off before he could finish, throwing him from his chair and launching him into the cockpit wall beside him, his bulky frame briefly crumpling into a state of semi-unconsciousness.

"MALLOK!!" Nate cried at his friend.

The Deesher was quick to his feet, albeit clearly disorientated, as he haphazardly dragged himself back into his chair. He wasn't the kind to show fear often, but his bald, blue head flooded with perspiration, and his black, circular eyes revealed far more than they usually would. He knew enough about space travel to know that those who were unlucky enough to stumble onto an unstable hyperlane were usually never seen again, and those that survived were so badly scarred, both mentally and physically, by the encounter that they often never flew again.

"Like I was saying," he panted as he tried desperately to reconfigure the ship's pattern of travel, "we haven't done anything any differently. We put in the co-ordinates the same as we always would. No slip ups, no nothing. We've done nothing out of the ordinary. There's only one explanation for this!"

"Oh, I know!" Nate barked upon hearing Mallok's last sentence. "I'm trying to cling on to what hope I have that there's some other ludicrous explanation!"

"Yeah, well if I were you, I'd direct some of that hopeful energy towards remembering some of the survival stories we've heard over the years!"

"I never thought I'd need to worry about it!"

Nate quickly jumped out of his chair and staggered to the back of the ship, leaving Mallok alone as the latter continued to try and resolve this through tinkering away at the console in front of him.

Nothing was working!

Suddenly, he heard a serious of bangs from where Nate had headed off to. Some of them sounded like a Human fist pounding away at infrastructure, others sounded more like mini explosions. The latter appeared to be confirmed as lights throughout the ship began to flicker and fade.

"Oh, no," was all Mallok could muster.

He continued to work away on the console, but to no avail, and as more of the ship's lights died, he soon found himself losing hope. The explanation Nate didn't want to address would have to be acknowledged now, with a further added problem. With the rest of the ship seemingly failing, but not dropping out of hyperspace, it could only mean that the ship had been tampered with. Combine that with being on an unstable hyperlane, and the chances of surviving this were dwindling rapidly.

Mallok dropped his head into his hands, both out of frustration as well as trying to think back to how they had blindly walked into this predicament. Thinking back to these past few weeks on Vuste, and the absolute chaos that had erupted between the settlements. The idea that the ship had been tampered with shouldn't be so surprising given everything that had happened, but the opportunity for any tampering couldn't possibly have taken place without it arousing their suspicion. Nobody they didn't already know had gone near the ship!

"Mallok!"

Nate was suddenly back in the cockpit, fear & anger battling for the right to dominate the look he expressed on his face.

The Deesher whipped his head up to face him, his own anxieties clear as day. "Tell me it's not been screwed around with," he barked at the Human, almost begging for the right answer.

"We've been done over," Nate replied in exasperation. "Somebody has stitched us over. I can't override it, there's no way I can pull us out of hyperspace without blowing the whole thing to pieces. Everything else has just capitulated. I don't understand..."

Mallok returned his head into his palms.

"There's been no one on this ship that we don't know," he said, the sound muffled through his hands. "Who's done this?"

After a moment's pause, Nate asked "Who gave us the co-ordinates?"

"What?"

"The co-ordinates. Who gave them to us?"

Even more exasperated, Mallok asked "Why would the co-ordinates matter if the ship's screwed?"

"Because even with a screwed-up ship, somebody else could drag us out of hyperspace using a strong enough vessel," Nate answered. "It wasn't enough to simply bugger the ship, we were given those co-ordinates to make sure we couldn't survive!"

Mallok's face took on a blank expression momentarily while he considered Nate's theory, and he glanced back towards the console.

"But that doesn't explain the sabotage, we'd dealt with everybody who could be a problem on Vuste."

Slumping himself into his chair but keeping his eyes on his old friend, Nate asked again "Mallok, who gave us the co-ordinates?"

"The same as ever!" the Deesher answered, losing patience with every passing second. "The little fella, the old guy's friend. But he's always come through before whenever we've been on Vuste, what could've changed now?"

Leaning back into his chair as he eyeballed the distorted stars outside the cockpit window, Nate gripped his jaw in his hand as he tried to figure everything out.

"Did he say anything specifically about the co-ordinates?"

"I asked him for somewhere quiet," Mallok explained. "Especially after everything back there, I said we needed somewhere to drift for a while. He said he'd been given a tip-off by one of the old guy's visitors."

A cold rush suddenly ran through Nate, as he lifted his head from his hand and glanced back at Mallok.

"Visitors? But he's only had one..."

Mallok was quickly on his wavelength.

"That one with the elongated head! What did the old man call him, 'The Magister'?"

"That's it! Said he'd known him for years but he popped by every now and again! And he was the one who gave the little fella the co-ordinates?"

"It must've been! But that doesn't explain all this!"

Or, at least, Mallok didn't want to dive right into the conclusion that Nate had already silently made. The old man was a conundrum in himself; any visitors he had would have to be of some importance, especially given everything the old man knew!

"Mallok..."

"Nate, don't say it. Please, don't say it."

"We've been stabbed in the back! The little fella was on this ship before we left, correct?"

"Yep, to make sure the ship was good to go."

The two of them slumped further into their chairs, Nate covering his face with his left hand while Mallok gripped his skull in frustration. The former thought he heard something... elsewhere, for a moment, and seemed to lose himself, but it quickly passed.

The cockpit was silent for a few minutes, as cruel inevitability began to achieve acceptance by the two men within it.

"I'm so sorry, Nate."

"Behave!" the Human barked. "You're like a brother to me, you know my policy; don't ever apologise to me for anything! Our luck had to run out some day."

"But after everything we've been through. How have we been done like this?"

"Whoever 'The Magister' was, he clearly had an agenda."

Nate's disgust was quickly subsiding as he became more and more accepting of his fate. Like he said, their luck had to run out someday. And what a way to go...

"We're going out with a bang, Mallok!"

The Deesher looked over to his friend with sadness in those black eyes, but a wry smile slowly grew on his face.

"Would we have it any other way?"

"Not a chance!"

With that, Nate swung his chair around and cracked open an old cabinet where two small glasses were kept with some fine whiskey.

Oblivion awaited. There was no better way to face it than with a toast and a celebration of all they'd been through.

Nate filled the glasses and passed one to his friend, before the two gave them a clank and downed the contents.

"Bah! I always said this stuff was like the fiery death! The bitter irony!" Mallok boomed. "Another?"

"Another!" Nate howled as he complied. Before he took his swig, however, he paused to contemplate something. Mallok noticed this, and he too paused his swig.

"Penny for your thoughts?"

Nate chuckled, and replied "I think you can guess."

Mallok gave a chuckle of his own with a little nod. "Yeah, I can. Can I raise a toast with you?"

"You don't have to ask, fella!"

The two raised their glasses, clanked them again and called out in unison "To Zannah!" before downing the whiskey.

Zannah.

Nate's great love. Her image took control of his mind. So often he had struggled with her loss, but he was at peace now. And he'd be seeing her again. Soon.

As Mallok let out a series of ineligible yet comical noises after that second intake of the whiskey, Nate whispered "I'm coming home, babe."

The distorted star lines outside the ship began to warp even further. Mere seconds remained, but the two friends embraced it, as Mallok let out a rallying cry of his people, while Nate let out a wild howl of his own. They met their fates without apology.

The unstable hyperlane completely collapsed and the ship crashed into oblivion!

TO BE CONTINUED...

The Man In The Mansion

"Still wasting your life away, Mr. Tom?"

An old voice passing judgement as ever. Like being in a small-town eating house and having the waiter trying to pass on philosophical advice while he slaves his life away on less than pittance wages.

Tom slowly swirled his whiskey glass around, his fingers gripped around the rim, his hand moving as though in a hypnotic motion as the contents whipped around inside.

"You can't waste away a life when you don't have one to begin with," Tom muttered bitterly. "You of all people should know that."

A weak and tired smile crept across the face of the old butler.

"Yes, sir," he replied, "I suppose I should, having dedicated my life to this house and its many inhabitants for so long."

"Hmph, I'd say it stopped being a service a long time ago," the younger man snarled.

"Well, I avoided the use of the term 'service' for good reason, Mr. Tom."

Tom kept silent upon hearing that, instead feeling his body give off a little shudder. He fixated his gaze instead into the crackling fire, which in itself seemed to possess more life than anything else in this godforsaken house. Not that it was a regular house, of course. No, this was a mansion, and an old one at that. Very old. It had belonged to Tom's family for centuries, and at different times had played host to a wide variety of gatherings, some of incredible importance, others of dubious excess and others still of simple family reunion. Now, however...

"Something on your mind, Mr. Tom?"

The old butler almost peered into Tom's soul, as his old body appeared cocked to one side slightly as he cheerfully gazed at the younger man. Tom's eyes shifted to view the butler, a look of half-confusion and half-disgust on his face as he pondered how to respond. That was often the problem when engaging with the butler; never knowing what to say. It would be a most curious thing, were it not so infuriating.

Dropping his eyes back to the flames, Tom replied "Just finding myself lost in my appreciation of this fire, wondering how nature's features possess the ability to consume with such ease."

The butler's smile grew slightly, as he too turned to gaze at the fire.

"An old relative of yours was like that," he said. "The Grand gentleman, Ulysses. Incredibly thoughtful in his approach, and even more thought-provoking in his discourse. A shame you never had the opportunity to converse with him. I imagine he could've been somewhat of a mentor to you."

"Ah well, such is life," Tom mumbled, dismissively.

Maintaining his wry smile, the butler paused for a moment before turning on his heel and leaving Tom to his thoughts. As he did, Tom glanced as the older man left the room. Occasionally, he felt guilty for being so abrupt with him, but then he reminded himself of his predicament, and then simply returned to a state of disgust and loathing. Not necessarily at the gentleman, more just at life itself. He took a sip of his whiskey, and gazed around as the crackling fire gave off enough light to allow him to examine the room in at least some kind of detail. Old paintings adorned the walls, featuring relatives and ancestors going back far longer than Tom cared to think about, although he found a small bit of appreciation for the fact that, in thanks to their service, his family had sanctioned paintings of the various staff who had served them over the centuries. The most recent, of course, was that of the gentleman who had just left the room.

To his credit, he carried quite an elegant pose when required to, despite simultaneously appearing incredibly modest. A cheerful smile was etched on his aged face, his white, receded hairline combed and tucked in neatly around his cranium, with a spotless, creaseless white towel rested over his left arm and his silk gloved hands rested delicately just across his ribcage area. Again, a nagging hint of guilt rippled through Tom at his callous treatment of the man...

"On a guilt trip are we, Tom?"

A nagging guilt that dissolved into a puddle of acidic bile.

"I was," he mumbled, taking another sip, "and then you arrived."

"Hmph! I would've thought you'd appreciate the company..."

"I'd more appreciate the company of Death," he remarked sardonically, "and to be fair, that's not entirely meant sarcastically..."

A woman, whom the new voice belonged to, stepped into his line of sight. The mansion's librarian, her appearance would suggest the woman to be in her late forties or so, and Tom could never rid himself of the suspicion that had she kept herself presentable, she would probably be a uniquely attractive woman. Alas, she gave no care to presentation, as her brown hair was left unkept, her clothes seemingly unwashed, her general demeanour left to wane.

"And now you're once again wondering how different I could look," the woman sneered, immediately allowing her amusement to show as Tom's face exposed his surprise.

"For just how long have you been peering into my thoughts, exactly?" he asked with a combined hint of alarm & concern. "And why didn't I know about this earlier?"

Letting out a peevish giggle, the woman replied "Oh Tom, I can't read your thoughts. I simply read your face. An expression, however plain or powerful, can reveal an entire book's worth of thoughts and feelings. Some can hide their inner voice quite well, while others, like yourself, struggle to do so. I'm simply a good reader, nothing more and nothing less. You can't beat a good book, after all..."

"So, I suppose I should start sleeping in the library then?" Tom asked, sarcastically.

"If you'd like," she answered in mock innocence. "I could read you some bedtime stories and keep you warm, as well."

"Alternatively, you could just leave me alone," Tom remarked as he shuddered at the woman's sartorial offer. "This whiskey gives me all the warmth I need."

Turning her nose up, she said "That's your problem, Tom. You've locked yourself away, bitter and twisted, when all you really need is to allow yourself to be free. Wriggle free of those chains and be happy. But no, you simply rest there in that chair of yours and drink yourself silly."

"Ah, but I have a gift," he retorted. "I never get drunk, so I need never worry about all the negative side effects. The drink deals with all the negatives I struggle to deal with on my own. All these chains you reference are unlockable, but the drink allows me to ignore the pain inflicted by the vice grip they possess."

"I never said letting go would be a painless exercise," the woman said, quite serious all of a sudden. "But in order to be free or to reach an ideal end goal, we must often encounter pain. Surely you must realise this."

"Surely *you* must realise that I'm a lost cause, my dear," Tom replied. Downing his drink and setting the glass on the small table beside him, he grabbed the nearby bottle and began to pour himself a top-up. Once he was satisfied with the amount in his glass, he turned back to the woman and said "I do applaud your efforts, though. Indeed, I even appreciate them. However, I appreciate the butler even more, for he knows when to walk away. You never do, hence my irritance at your company. A shame really, for I honestly *do* love a good book."

A look of disgust briefly lingered on the woman's face, before it evaporated and was replaced by one of defeat. Letting out a sigh, her eyes gave Tom an up-and-down inspection, before she clumsily turned on her heel and, like the butler before her, began to leave the room.

"I'll be in the library," she barked as she left.

"Expect a late return..." Tom mumbled in response, gazing aimlessly into his glass. Suddenly finding himself weary of the drink, he set it to one side and lumbered himself up from the chair, giving himself a quick dust down with the backs of his hands, and he too began to stroll towards the doorway, albeit with a rather lazier demeanour than the ones shown by the butler and the librarian. Once at the doorway itself, he stopped and dipped his head through it ever so slightly, looking to his left, and then to his right, hoping to avoid any immediate fresh company. He'd rather just wander around by his lonesome for the time being, however long that may be.

He decided to turn right, seeing as both the butler and the librarian had turned left if he wasn't mistaken, and made his way towards the stairway facing the old front door. Before taking the intended turn to begin making his way upstairs, he found himself intrigued by the door momentarily, and wondered if he needed a quick flurry of fresh air. It seemed awfully black outside, but maybe a cold breeze with a dash of starlight could lift some of the weight from his shoulders. However, as he went to open the door, he found it locked. Not simply locked where you would be able to give the door a bit of a shake, but fully jammed. The door wouldn't budge at all.

Eh? Tom thought to himself absently.

Not even the slightest movement. As though cemented in place. For the briefest moment, a hint of fear rushed through Tom, until it rapidly subsided, as though deep down he knew why it wouldn't budge. But he remained somewhat baffled as to why it wouldn't. Whether the whiskey had nullified his ability to care, however, he couldn't say, but he simply shrugged at the development, and turned back to the stairs and began to climb them. As he did, he glanced to his right, noticing more paintings. Some of them had actually been painted by some of his ancestors, and though he had often been quite ignorant towards art, he had to admire their efforts. Some of them were simple in their meaning but pleasant all the same, such as portraits of the countryside. Others, however, seemed to possess a different kind of character. Some were of gatherings, such as those of seemingly incredible importance.

But they carried a darkness to them, and Tom couldn't quite determine why. He couldn't help but feel that the meetings that had taken place had had far reaching consequences, with decisions made by men in suits with dark and disturbing ambitions and goals, with no care for those impacted by such decisions who in turn would never know such meetings had ever taken place. And indeed, the painted representations of these dark figures seemed to be almost...

Alive would be the wrong word, but it certainly felt that a hint of their souls had been left behind in this old mansion. Maybe that's what lingered on Tom's shoulders. A darkness left behind that had afflicted this place over the centuries. He found himself lost in his ponderances, until...

"Ah, so you've remembered that this place has more than just a ground floor!"

The booming voice of the house chef met Tom's ears like an unwelcome morning bell, and the younger man stopped dead in his tracks as he felt his face slump in disappointment.

"I never forgot, you old fool," he bit out. "I simply preferred the company of the fire and the whiskey. Double heat packs a pleasant punch, I'll have you know. Anyway, why are you up here?"

"I got lost," the chef replied, completely deadpan, the comic smile he had previously worn suddenly falling flat, lost behind his bushy moustache.

"Lost?" Tom echoed in bemusement. "You've known this place like the back of your hand since before I was born."

"Memory isn't what it once was, young Tom," the chef explained in seeming honesty. "You know how it is."

"That would explain why the standard of the food has dipped to an utterly appalling standard," Tom replied sardonically. "That is, whenever the food is actually made. Do your staff need fresh training or have they all gone mad?"

"Couldn't honestly say," the chef shrugged, his eyes popping wide for a moment. "I haven't seen them since I came up here."

"And how long ago was that?" Tom asked, his eyebrows cocking.

"About twenty years ago, I think," the chef answered.

Irritated, Tom sighed to himself, feeling a sudden desire to allow himself to fall back down the stairs and put himself out of his misery.

"I'm not in the mood for this idiocy," he grumbled.

"No?" the chef replied. "Ah well, be seeing you around, Mr. Tom."

With that, the chef suddenly began walking down the corridor, although where to couldn't be determined. He seemed to be walking directly into the dark.

"Where are you going?" Tom asked, calling after him.

"Couldn't honestly say..." the chef's voice boomed back, as his physical body appeared to be consumed by the darkness.

A grim feeling crept up Tom's spine as he gazed into the black space which the chef had drifted into. Suddenly feeling as though upstairs was to be strictly avoided, and wondering if he preferred to remain grounded for a reason, Tom turned and made his way back downstairs. Once he reached the bottom, he was tempted to make another attempt to open the front door, but a part of him seemed to tell him not to bother, lest he be further baffled by his futile attempts. He lost any enthusiasm for wandering around the house any further, and decided to return to his chair by the fire. Better to allow the whiskey to consume him than petty bemusements & creepy unknowns.

When he returned to the room in question that contained his chair and whiskey, however, he noticed that the crackling fire appeared... dimmer. As though time had passed without someone stoking it to ensure it sustained its life. Tom gazed into the fireplace, a scowl of sorts growing on his face. He walked over to it, picking up the prodder by its side once he reached it, and began to try and give the flames a boost.

Nothing seemed to happen.

Staring blankly into the fire, Tom put the prodder back in its place, and slumped into his chair, his eyes not leaving the light emanating from the fireplace. Continuing to stare into the fire, he absently went for his glass of whiskey, only to discover that it was missing. Quickly moving his gaze from the fire to the little table next to the chair, he found that both the glass and the bottle had been moved.

Growling to himself, Tom called out "BUTLER!"

"Yes, Sir?"

Whipping his head around in shock, clearly not expecting the old gentleman to have answered so quickly, nor to be standing at the doorway, Tom spat "Jesus wept! How long have you been stood there?!?"

"Since you called, Mr. Tom," the butler answered, a gentle smile on his face.

"That was literally just now!" Tom barked in bafflement.

"Indeed, it was," the old man replied. "And here I am. How can I help you?"

Tom froze for a moment, but as he was about to gather himself and vociferously ask the butler where the bloody hell his whiskey had gone, he suddenly noticed something about the old man.

He had aged. He had aged years.

He was old before, but now he appeared close to death's door.

Impossible, he had just seen him barely ten minutes or so earlier.

"What's wrong, Mr. Tom?" the butler asked, noticing the younger man's confusion.

"What happened to you?" Tom asked in response. "You've... aged!"

Chuckling, the butler replied "Well, I've been around a fair old while, Sir. Age tends to catch up with you."

"Something isn't right," Tom said, a sense of concern growing on his face and in his voice. "Something's not right at all."

"Everything's absolutely fine, Mr. Tom," the butler said, assuringly.

Tom began to feel a hint of madness infect him, and it only grew worse when he looked the old man in the face. Looking back to the fire for an alternative, he saw it begin to slowly fade.

"Why is the fire dying like this?" he asked in alarm, chewing his thumb as he watched the flames weaken.

"All things die, Mr. Tom," the butler answered quietly.

Tom turned his face back to the butler, about to spit out something about being irritated by the old man's philosophical whims.

Whatever he intended to say never escaped his throat, as he found himself locked in horror at the appearance of the butler. His eyes were gone, his sockets simply black and empty.

His aged skin had rotted and sunken close to the bone.

His gentle smile held barely in place, very weak and very sad.

"Goodbye, Mr. Tom."

And with that, the corpse-like figure of the old butler simply disintegrated into dust.

After what felt like an eternity of silence, a noise suddenly escaped from Tom's mouth that sounded like a terrified shriek and a mortified howl blended into one.

Tom remained in his chair, his hands gripping onto the ends of the arms as though holding on for dear life. He stared at where the butler had stood, as the dust that had gathered after his disintegration appeared to simply disappear. A new, undefinable fear suddenly took a grip on Tom's psyche. Unable to efficiently gather his thoughts, he remained fixed in the chair for an undeterminable length of time.

As he did, the fire continued to die.

Eventually, something gathered within Tom that enabled him to rise from the chair. He paused for a moment, his face still wearing a look of horror, as he gazed down at where the dust no longer was.

Suddenly deciding he needed to move, his quickly made his way out of the room, and this time turned left, not even wanting to look right at the immovable front door. Instead, he darted down a long corridor, and eventually found himself at the mansion's library.

Not a conventional library, of course, but certainly one that would trigger envy in most hearts. At its peak, this small library played host not only to a huge array of texts, but also acted as a place of study for members of the mansion's family. Members of all ages in fact, from youngsters studying the ways of the world, to great minds looking to achieve mastery in their respective fields. Now, however, this library lay dormant. The old texts remained, but the majority of them hadn't been opened for many a year, and a dinginess wore heavily on the room's atmosphere. A dinginess that threatened to consume Tom immediately upon entry.

"At last, you come to me, Tom," the librarian's voice called out from the dark with cruel mockery. "You've kept me waiting for far too long."

"I'm not here for games, woman!" he bit back. "The butler is dead!"

"I know," she replied. "He served so well. A treasure not only to this place, but to all those who have inhabited it. None more so than you."

The library was lit up only slightly thanks to sconces that were scattered across the walls, a hazardous approach one would've thought given the presence of books. Regardless, the woman came out of the dark just enough to be seen by Tom, and as before, he found himself shocked at the change of appearance. Whereas earlier the woman looked to be in her late forties or so, now she looked to be at least two decades older, if not more. Worse still, she still looked like she hadn't washed. Peculiarly, no smell seemed to linger from her. Tom took the briefest moment to appreciate that bizarre feature.

"What's wrong, Tom?" she asked, although her face wore a look that said that she already knew.

Tom failed to answer, and as such the woman allowed herself a chuckle, as she moved slightly closer to him.

"This place haunts you, doesn't it, dear?" she queried, again already knowing the answer.

"Something's wrong," Tom replied, although the words themselves carried very little meaning. He didn't really know what to say at all.

"Something has been wrong with this place for an awfully long time, Tom," the woman said rather thoughtfully. "It has left its crude mark on many who came before you, and now you are the end of the line."

"End of the line?" Tom echoed. "What do you mean?"

Chuckling again, the woman answered "Oh, come on, Tom. You're the last member of this historical bloodline. All of your relatives are gone, you never married nor produced offspring. You are the last in this place, and as such you are the one who bears witness as its infection runs its course."

"You see, Tom, this old mansion played host to a family that prided itself on greatness. It demanded the absolute best from every generation it spawned, hoping to produce the finest minds and creators no matter the cost nor repercussion. It wined and dined the world's powers, spreading its influence wherever possible. It gathered wealth like no one could possibly imagine. But in the end, this bloodline fell victim to a backlash. You see, when you steep to such dark depths, influencing the lives of millions, trying to stretch beyond the boundaries of nature, inevitably nature will strike back. Over time, your family's wealth, influence and indeed numbers whittled away. Less and less offspring were born, and those who *were* born were often afflicted by horrific mental health. Such as yourself, my dear."

Tom staggered to a chair nearby, and slumped down into it, rubbing his hand over his face. Once he had finished ruffling his face, he looked back at the woman, who continued to gaze at him in return, though there was no malice in her face whatsoever.

"All things come to an end, Tom," she continued. "It's just that, as a result of your family's actions, its legacy is one of bastardisation, and those who carry the lineage to its end must suffer the consequences. That's where we, those who served your family, have tried to help. In serving your family, we too fell under the affliction, and so we must suffer alongside you, but we do so with the intent of ensuring you are never alone. Yes, we annoy you a little bit, but we can take the brunt of that, as long as we are doing our duties."

"It makes no sense..." was all Tom could say.

"It makes all the sense in the world," the woman chortled. "At least, when one's mind is at ease. And unfortunately, yours never is, but we're here for you, and we will be until this all eventually ends."

"When what ends?" Tom asked.

"This," the woman replied, gently waving her hands around. "When this place is finally allowed to die. It might not be for some time yet, but that time will come eventually. Anyway, I better be off."

The woman turned and began to stroll back into the darkness.

"Where are you going?" Tom asked, stopping her in her tracks.

Turning back to face him, her eyes seeming to age by the second, she replied "I'm *going*, Tom. Don't worry, this'll end eventually." She took a look around the library, an almost disgruntled look across her face. "Eventually."

And with that, she turned again, but before Tom could call to her, her footsteps abruptly ceased, and Tom saw speckles of dust escape the dark and fall into the light. The same kind of speckles that were left behind when the butler disintegrated earlier.

Tom froze again, and again it felt like an eternity until he could gather himself. There was a sense of... similarity about all this. As though he was beginning to feel a sense of Déjà vu, as though he had witnessed these speckles before, been baffled and terrified in equal measure by how they had come to be.

Whereas earlier he felt gripped by fear, now he felt gripped by cold. He rose from the chair, and slowly backed out of the library, before turning back down the corridor towards the immovable front door.

Immovable front door...

Never to be unlocked, never to allow those inside to inhale clean air and see the stars again. Immovable, with those locked behind condemned.

Condemned...

The woman's words suddenly found an element of clarity, and again a sense of familiarity. Remembering the paintings of the meetings of great importance, Tom turned left with the intent of looking once more at the paintings that hung on the stairwell, maybe hoping to see the faces of the men whose actions had condemned this place and its inhabitants, but instead he saw somebody waiting for him.

The chef.

"Ah, Mr. Tom!" he boomed. "How are you?"

The chef, like the butler and the librarian, had also aged, his bushy moustache now a snowy white, with tired bags under his eyes.

"Where've you been?" Tom asked bluntly.

"No idea, I think I got lost," the chef chirped. "Listen, I'm on my way to the kitchen, how about that last meal?"

He seemed so blasé, as though there was absolutely nothing irregular about all of this.

As though it was all going to plan.

Wait, what?

"Last meal?" Tom blurted out. "What last meal?"

"You know, your last meal," the chef replied. "The last one I make for you."

Tom seemed to mumble something incoherent, his eyes almost wearing a look of incredulity.

Enjoying a chuckle to himself, the chef said "Not to worry, Mr. Tom! I'll pop down to the kitchen now and get it all sorted out. You sit yourself down by the fire. I doubt there's much of it left."

And with that, off he went down the corridor and eventually towards the kitchen, wherever it was. Tom had long forgotten, now he considered it.

Looking back at the immovable door momentarily, before turning back to head towards the room where his chair awaited him, he found his body feeling somewhat weaker. Dare he say it, he felt rather aged.

He soon found his way back to his chair and slumped himself down, where he assumed the chef would be with him shortly to serve this 'last meal.' It dawned on him for a split second that he wasn't actually challenging any of this, he was simply going along with it, but then he thought nothing more of it and carried on, waiting for his meal.

And, indeed, the chef soon arrived with his meal on a tray. Bread.

Just bread, lightly coated with finely salted butter.

"So, this is it, is it?" Tom asked with a mumble as he gazed at the bread in bafflement. "The last meal..."

"Well, we'll have to wait and see won't we, my friend," the chef cheerfully replied.

"What do you mean?" Tom asked, looking up at him.

Letting out an amused puff, the chef answered "It's not exactly the first time, Mr. Tom. Anyway, no more questions, may your bread be blessed and may you find a little bit of peace."

Indeed, the chef allowed for no more questions, as he stepped back, folded his hands behind his back and gave a respectful bow.

"Bye for now, Mr. Tom!"

And then, he too, disintegrated.

Once again, Tom took an eternity to get his bearings right, but when he eventually did, he lifted his arms over the tray that lay across his lap and began to consume his bread. It was pleasant, he was happy to say. So pleasant in fact that he had been so caught up in enjoying the bread that he hadn't noticed something about his hands.

They were old hands. Delicate and frail, with liver spots showing. He hadn't simply *felt* aged earlier when he strolled into the room, he *had* aged. More Déjà vu, he realised as he gazed at his digits. He *had* seen this before. The chef had even alluded to it. So had the librarian in fact. Even the butler.

What was it the chef had said about the last meal?

It's not exactly the first time...

What was it the librarian had said?

We're here for you, and we will be until this all eventually ends...

And the butler? Reminiscing of Ulysses and how this had long stopped being a 'service.'

This was happening over and over and over and over again. He, Tom, was the last of the lineage of this mansion's family. And he was condemned for the sins of those who had come before, and these people who kept him company had been condemned too, but were staying by his side to make sure he was never alone. He wasn't exactly appreciative though, was he. Then again, he thought himself as just a regular thirty-year-old surrounded by people who found solace in servitude, and he had never understood that. Not until they were all gone, and he had realised that they were all in this together.

Now that he thought about it, he wondered just how many times this had happened.

On top of that, how did the servants know it was happening but he didn't until they were all gone?

He supposed answers to such questions were unachievable. Although, they did remind him of some old tales. He slowly, and painfully, turned his old head to gaze back at the fire, which was now almost gone completely. He realised that the fire was representative of his life. Maybe that was why he was so drawn to it.

As he remembered the tales, he tried to find his voice, wondering if maybe those who had left him would be able to hear him. Whether they would answer was irrelevant, he just wanted to say something. Eventually he spoke, albeit with a voice he didn't fully recognise. A bit of his character was there, but it was old, crackly and weak. Like the fire.

"I'm reminded of tales of the dark scientist with the bulbous features, and of the doctor who spent an eternity looking for answers. These men who achieved great things but were hindered by sins, either of their own doing or of the doing of others. Men who lived and died over and over again, wondering when it would end."

There came no answer, but he didn't mind. He simply hoped that his company might hear his reflective words, and maybe give a little smile at his attempts at old, philosophical wisdom.

He wondered to himself whether this was the last time he would have to endure this, or whether it was all part of a greater lesson he had yet to truly learn from.

Maybe he needed to learn a little bit of decency, a little bit of respect. Maybe he just needed closure.

As the fire faded away and finally died, so did Tom, his body disintegrating and crumbling into dust as had been the case for those who had kept him company.

His final thoughts were not entirely peaceful, but certainly they contained hope that this was the last time he would go through this. If not, he at least hoped that he would have taken one step closer to the end.

***

"Still wasting your life away, Mr. Tom?"

An old voice passing judgement as ever. Like being in a small-town eating house and having the waiter trying to pass on philosophical advice while he slaves his life away on less than pittance wages.

Tom slowly swirled his whiskey glass around, his fingers gripped around the rim, his hand moving as though in a hypnotic motion as the contents whipped around inside.

"You can't waste away a life when you don't have one to begin with," Tom muttered bitterly. "You of all people should know that..."

The Reunion

I have waited a long time for this day.

Far too long, in fact. Twenty years have passed since my school days came to an end. I recall the joy I felt that the twelve years of misery & strife were finally over, foolishly believing that I was about to embark on a positive new journey in life. Yes, I actually believed that life was to get better, even though a part of me was terrified by the prospect of adulthood. I suppose my mindset was focused on the principle of "anything must be better than living with the chains of school." Once my time there was over, the chains I had worn for all but four years of my life were broken, and I was "free!"

Hmph, "freedom." I suppose I could go on a rant about the complexities of freedom, and what it truly means, but I have far more important things on my mind.

You see, though the last twenty years have been rather vile in their own way, the chains I referred to have never truly been cast aside. Yes, they were broken upon my departure from school, but I've continued to drag them around with me. No doubt you would probably judge me for being bogged down by such an issue, but I care not for judgement anymore. Not after what will transpire today.

The idea for this day actually came to me during those schooldays. Ironically enough, it was those around me, those who would mock me day after day with such relentless spite, who actually planted the seeds in my head which have been slowly developing for the last two decades. Today is not simply something conjured up out of nowhere and thrown together with nothing but hope, like launching shit at a wall and hoping it sticks. No, no, no, today will be the culmination of a plan that I would return to every so often over the years, meticulously pieced together with the intention of bringing it all to fruition at just the right time. Twenty years feels like the right time. After all, School Year reunions are always easier to throw when there's a sizeable anniversary attached to them.

First things first, of course, I needed a suitable location, and I have managed to snag my prime choice, the location I always had in mind; the Assembly Halls of the very school we attended. What better place to bring everyone together again! What better place for this reunion to end all reunions! What better place for the culmination of the grand plan!

In all fairness, securing the halls for the get together was relatively easy. The current figureheads seemed relatively eager to show off the school in its current state to those who had served ti-..., I mean, attended there in years gone by. Quite egotistical I thought. A headmaster wanting to make it all about their achievements, hardly surprising of course yet irritating all the same. My history with headmasters was a checkered one, admittedly, although generally it was far better than my history with their underlings. I did meet *some* teachers & headteachers who were genuinely good people, thankfully. Often, I found that the headteachers who were widely criticized or loathed by staff & students were usually the best, while those who received applause and commendation were those who could smile with ease and knife you even quicker. Teachers, of course, were a different kettle of fish. Criticism & acclaim for teachers often came from different kinds of students based off of their own experiences, and the shallow nature of people meant that their favour towards certain teachers would often fluctuate based on minor occurrences. I always found that to be both petty and distasteful. Such a fair-weather approach is never a positive feature in a person, and the presence of such a feature only increased my loathing for those around me. As if their false smiles & laughs didn't soil the air enough, as if their putrid personas didn't reflect the increasingly sour state of the next generation, as if their pathetically naïve & blinded viewpoints weren't completely obnoxious. Nope, just when you thought you couldn't hate them anymore, you find another reason to do so. It happened to me on a daily basis, and still, I can taste the bitterness at the back of my throat.

Admittedly, I must almost thank them. In the latter months of my schooldays, I developed more of a thicker skin, torn in places admittedly, but thicker. As such, I was able to stroll through without their poisonous ways completely butchering my day or mood, and it is this thick skin that I have been able to put to tremendous use throughout adulthood, albeit not always with success. Then again, I wonder if by that point in my school life whether I had already subconsciously made the decision to bring about this day. It would certainly explain how I was able to get by in those later days.

Anyway, fast forward to my planning.

The Assembly Halls secured, the school itself had the decency to inform me that they would open the on-site bar for the event, whilst also ensuring that all other food and drink requirements would be met by existing staff. I must admit, the presence of a bar in a school always bemused me, and I never truly found out how and why it had found itself onto the premises. Located just outside the main changing rooms and sports hall, it was a small bar much like those typically seen in a pub, complete with the usual variety of beverages and snacks on offer. Once or twice, you could even see a couple of people perched on seats at this bar, though whether these were caretakers & cleaners making use of the facilities during a break or outsiders who were allowed to drop in, I never did find out. Now that I think about it, in the midst of discussing my plans for my old school colleagues and indeed the premises itself, I find myself acknowledging not only the ludicrousness of a bar being on schoolgrounds, but just how ludicrous it must sound that such a thing even exists.

But exists it does, you have my word on that.

So, premises booked and all the essentials provided without me needing to deal with the latter separately. Now all was needed were the guests of honour. Modern means of communication allowed me to promote the event with consummate ease, and to make things even easier for me, my old class "mates" didn't even bother to pay attention to the fact that the person who had published the pages for this event on various social media platforms didn't even exist. I didn't fancy potentially botching all this hard work only for these pillocks to not turn up after seeing my name on the event invites. Funny, social media never was my cup of tea, hence why I avoided it, but in my hour of need, it has shown itself to have its uses. I don't wish to jinx myself, but from what I can gather, having promoted the event on these various platforms, attendance for the reunion could well hit 100%. I daren't allow myself to dream, not yet, but this day could be greater than I ever anticipated!

The hours have ticked by slowly today, as the event draws ever nearer, but I have waited long enough for this day to arrive, so the matter of a few short hours is hardly something to be mithered by.

I dropped by the school a short time ago very briefly, just to see that everything was prepared. I had to put on something of a façade for the school staff who are kindly dedicating their free time to this event, emphasizing my thanks for their efforts and the fact that they have brought all this to fruition.

Dare I say it, I almost feel guilty knowing what's to come.

Now, however, I find myself casually relaxing on the school fields. I took a walk around the school after meeting with the staff, allowing myself one last trip down memory lane. Some would undoubtedly giddily point to certain parts of the school and wax lyrical about their memories of certain occasions, but instead I simply had my inner monologue for company, remembering countless moments of embarrassment, humiliation, ridicule and, at times, downright torture. I was surprised at the amount of free reign I had, but given that the school is shut at the moment for half-term break, and that the current staff in charge are just so eager to combine the present with the past, they clearly had no qualms allowing me to make the most of my time here.

I popped through various departments and specific classrooms as I wandered around. I reminded myself of my regrets, not only at the fact that I came here to begin with, but also the fact that I made countless poor decisions while I was here, particularly on an academic level.

Oh? You thought this was going to be one of those "woe is me" stories? Not at all! I know full well the mistakes I have made in life, and I made far too many of them here, particularly when it came to not putting my abilities to good use. I could've done so much more. I *should've* done so much more.

And, ultimately, I was at fault for me not doing so. I was broken during my time here. Arguably, I was broken before I even stepped through the gates for the first time. But even so, there was so much I could've achieved, and I didn't. That's where a major hint of bitterness lies with myself, a portion of my angst and hatred aimed inwardly.

However, whilst that hint of self-directed bitterness may be substantial, it must not be forgotten that a sizeable majority of my derision is saved for the guests of honour. Making my own mistakes is one thing; having my life made a living hell by these cretins for so long is something else entirely. The grudge I have held has only strengthened over the last twenty years, poisoning my innards in the process, and as I was strolling through the corridors of this old school, I was reminded of that. Though my physical self walked and gazed around, and though their physical selves will soon converge on this place, I found myself surrounded by the ghosts of our teen selves haunting me on every corridor. Thrown objects in the English department, surround mockery outside Graphics, routine humiliation near Maths. And let's just not discuss the Business department.

The air around me is quite liberating, threatening to cleanse me of all evils as the grand plan's fruition ruminates through my thoughts. It's like a battle of wills taking place on the battlefield of my very soul. I find myself appreciating the efforts of those who cry out for righteousness and all that is good, but despite this, I cheer on the opposition, hardwired to allow passion to rule and dictate. Though my soul will suffer the consequences, darkness must have its victory on this day.

There is no other way, it simply must be like this.

I will never know peace while this continues to eat away at me.

As the time grows nearer, I shift myself to a more private location. Nearby are some trees that will allow me to remain hidden for the majority of the evening, watching on from the moment the guests of honour arrive. If the guests ask just who it is that arranged all this, the staff will provide them with the false name they believe to be real, and in doing so will undoubtedly lead the guests to believe that one of their own is using the name as a ruse, as part of a game for a bit of fun, with the guessing game adding to the occasion and the revelation to come near the end. Let their ignorance and desire for constant highs, games and euphoria lead them to their downfall. They have never known better, nor will they ever.

The trees are my bodyguards, and seeing as they are so much more natural than humans, that puts me at ease. I am pleasantly surprised to find that I am not suffering any nervous feelings, nor doubts or worries. My mind, and my conscious, is clear, and that clarity is only strengthened once the first guests arrive.

A small band of them in fact. They must have decided to arrive together, and already they appear to be quite giddy. No doubt they have spent the last hour or so engaging in "pre-drinks," an excuse usually used by late-teens to get smashed before they even step outside the front door before embarking on a night of hedonism. Though revolting, such scenes create a sight you can't quite take your eyes off. Hedonism is vile, yet nature is amazing.

Right on cue, more and more continue to arrive. Some, to their credit, are quite reserved, while others have clearly seen tonight as an opportunity to be who they once were. Maybe they never stopped being who they were and simply didn't realise.

While the majority have arrived by car or taxi, a small number appear to have walked. I'm reminded that many in my year used to live extremely close by, and it seems that some still do. Funny how that happens, how some so quickly depart from the neighbourhoods of their youth once the opportunity arises, while others remain where they feel they belong.

The contrast in their levels of prosperity over the past two decades seems to show through ever so slightly. Some dress to a respectable standard, not too flashy but certainly with a hint of elegance. Others tone it down further, possibly out of choice, possibly not. Others still expose their complete lack of class, either going overboard to the point of ludicrousness or simply looking abhorrently tacky.

As I assess the guests, arrival after arrival, I notice another small contrast; the body language on show.

Some have arrived with great exuberance, clearly eager to reunite with old friends. Then again, these people were often the kind who would dramatically embrace at the end of each school year only to spend almost every day with each other throughout the summer break.

Others, meanwhile, have arrived with a more reserved demeanour, clearly hoping to avoid bumping into certain people whilst quietly looking forward to spending time with old acquaintances.

The contrasting demeanours, much like the contrasting fashions, almost match what they were twenty years ago. In some way, every single one of these people remain who they were. By that I mean, a part of their sixteen-year-old selves remains unchanged. Of course, in many ways, they'll each be extremely different to who they were, but deep down they're still the same, and it's funny how upon their return to their old stomping ground, the part of them that has never changed almost returns to the surface. It should be no surprise then to see many of the old groupings and cliques coming together once more. Even if the respective members of these groupings and cliques have drifted apart over time, here they almost perform a sort of reunification, as though magnetized.

As more and more of them arrive, welcomed with such vigour by the current school staff, it slowly dawns on me that not a single figure is missing, a realisation soon confirmed. Attendance is indeed 100%. They are all here!

Everything truly is going as planned. Time to settle in for the moment, and allow them to enjoy their reunion while it lasts. Allow them to enjoy their brief euphoria, their temporary flurry of excitement, their little trip down memory lane.

I can see the lights coming from the windows of the Assembly Halls, and I can hear the music beginning to play, as a loud chatter of voices emanates from the scene of the gathering. I can also feel a small group of demons clawing up my shoulder blades, gripping on to my shoulders as they ascend, gasping viciously as they reach the top. Once there, their evil little chuckles are followed by their heinous encouragement.

What are you waiting for? they ask me. *The time is now!*

They are right, of course. The time is indeed now. The moment I have waited for, for so long, has finally arrived. But I will allow myself to bathe in this moment, just to consider everything that has led to it, and everything that is about to transpire. The company of these demons, too, I will also briefly focus on, as these are the final moments that they will spend with me. Good riddance, of course, I won't miss them, but they have been with me for so long, and knowing that they will soon be banished from my life leaves me focusing on them, as I must cherish their imminent exit and remind myself of why I am doing what I am about to do. It is all well and good achieving something, or fulfilling a duty, but if you do not appreciate why you are doing so and just what it truly means, then the achievement or the fulfillment will ultimately be tarnished. And so, I allow them to natter away to themselves on my shoulder, but I set them down on the floor before inhaling the evening air and setting forth once more towards the Assembly Halls. The demons cheer as I walk away, but I ignore them, too focused on the task at hand.

I think I know what you're probably suspecting at this point. That my intention is to burst in and surprise everyone, revealing myself as the grand planner, the great organiser, the one responsible for the show!

If you're of dark mind, you probably suspect that I will fling open the doors and unleash a great massacre, a bloodbath that I will swim in to bathe my soul!

If you're of a more innocent persuasion, maybe you're hoping I will indeed reveal myself, but in doing so I will flourish in the glory of the guests' surprise, putting my hatred to one side to instead join in and chuckle to myself as their shallow smiles are forced to stretch as they thank me for the get together. That's how I will win, you may be thinking, I will kill them with kindness!

If you fall into the latter category, then you're even further beyond help than I.

However, while there will be no cheerful reunion, there will also be no such bloodbath or massacre. At least, not in the demonic sense you may be fearing. My plan is far more discrete, and in a way, more philosophical and spiritual.

What I didn't tell you earlier was that I had locked the main exits leading from the halls back into the main area of the school, meaning they won't be able to go beyond the bar area. The guests won't see this as anything particularly peculiar if they happen upon the doors, after all they'll see no reason to go any further.

Once more, their ignorance will prove to be a hindrance to them.

Their only exit from the Assembly Halls will be the way they entered, through a large doorway facing the main road, while the fire exits have also been silently declared 'malfunctioned.' The large doorway itself, however, will never open again. The music acts as a wonderful sound cushion, I realise as I approach the door. Already shut, all that is required now is for the doors to be chain-locked. Not a soul inside hears as I ensure that the Halls will be their final destination, before I initiate the next phase.

Petrol. Lots and lots of petrol.

I quietly perched a number of small petrol tanks in key areas of the vicinity upon my arrival, prior to actually meeting with the staff, and they are in pole position to do maximum damage. First, however, a couple of them will be required to set the final stage of the grand plan into motion. I collect a couple of the tanks and begin to release their contents around the perimeter of the Halls, making sure I coat the outside walls just as much as I do the concrete floor, before eventually returning to the locked door and leaving a pool of petrol beside it.

The stage is set.

The various tanks will trigger even greater damage once the fire reaches them, and this whole place will be consumed. But a single match must first be lit, and that is my final duty.

I reach into my pocket and pull out an old box of matches, amused momentarily by their vintage design and smell. I slide open the box, picking a single match at random. I strike it along the side of the box, and a small flame is born at the top.

Big things have small beginnings.

I step back ever so slightly, and toss the match into the pool of petrol in front of the door, and almost instantaneously, the flames grow. Satisfied with the immediacy of the fire's growth, I turn and make my way back towards the trees where I waited so patiently earlier. As I walk, I can hear the intensity of the sound effects grow in the distance behind me, with the fire flickering and spitting in anger. I simply focus on returning to my spot, shadowed within the trees. That is what I have become, a shadow. This entire petty event was of my making, and the downfall of my alumni was my doing. Once I reach the trees, I pause for a moment, not immediately turning to face the school. Instead, I look around at the grass below me, and listen.

There is only the fire in the distance.

The demons, those nattering little bastards whose violent encouragements I took the time to savour earlier, are gone.

They are gone.

I afford myself the smallest of smiles, and *then* I turn to face the school.

To face the fire.

In doing so, I realise that I am suddenly a one-person audience of an opera that I have spent twenty years writing. Twenty years putting together my masterpiece, and now I can savour the fruits of my labour.

Then, the sounds I anticipated finally begin to be heard.

The screams.

Though the sounds of the fire consuming the Halls dominates the atmosphere, the screams of those inside are finally emanating from within. Horrible, tortured, fearful screams. Just like the ones I so wanted to unleash during my years of suffering here.

But look at this, this great masterpiece.

My old enemies and the stage that played host to their mockery, their theatre you could say. They are burning as one.

I've no doubt that a fire brigade will be here shortly, but it'll be too late for those inside, and I shall be gone by then. Their attempts, however admirable, will be in vain, for the symbol of this school, its Great Assembly Halls, will now be known as a graveyard for the damned souls of my enemies!

I gaze a little while longer from the distance, before I turn and head in the opposite direction. Where my future lies, I know not, and quite frankly, I care not!

I care only for one thing, and I notice it as I walk with such liberty.

My chains are no longer simply broken; they are finally discarded for good.

At last, I am free.

The Man With Nothing Left

"There's nowhere else to look, Inspector Mercer. We're up shit's creek with this one!"

Inspector Mercer had heard it all before, the defeatism of her colleagues. Far too willing to abandon ship and move on to the next, rather than buckle up and actually try and focus on the job at hand.

"That's bollocks and you know it!" Mercer bit back, her tired eyes burning for a brief moment. Seeing her young colleague's anguish at her response would usually have left her with a hint of guilt, but she felt none of it today. "I need something of substance. Find something, for Christ's sake!"

"But what exactly are we looking for, ma'am?" the young colleague in question, PC Jones, asked in desperation, clearly perplexed. "I don't wish to give up the ghost, but you know more than I do that some things just go unsolved. It completely goes against why we do the job, but we can't control everything. We've detailed every single crime scene there is, and nothing leads back to a killer. I've never seen anything like this before!"

"Yeah, well, there's a first time for everything, especially in this line of work," Mercer grumbled. Now forty-eight years of age, she has climbed the force's ladder with dignity, conviction and ethics. It has been a climb that has ultimately shattered her, leaving her proud at her achievements, but incredibly bitter at who she has become. She goes home to an empty house after each shift, no family there to welcome her with open arms. When she's on shift, her colleagues tread on egg shells around her, fearful of her vicious retorts too often dished out to officers who too often fall below acceptable standards. Her record demands respect, and her presence automatically brings it, but the spritely young officer of 20+ years ago is long gone. PC Jones, on the other hand, has just turned twenty-five, and though he has a relatively strong head on him, and undoubtedly possesses a body of principles built on wanting to do good, he is still engulfed by the kind of naivete that doesn't really leave an individual until they've escaped their twenties. He has been on the receiving end of Mercer's mood swings quite regularly lately, and though he keeps his chin up and gets on with the job, privately he wonders what exactly he can do to stay on the Inspector's good side. It is the young man's words, however, that suddenly leave Mercer in a state of reflection.

We've detailed every single crime scene there is, and nothing leads back to a killer. I've never seen anything like this before!

Jones hadn't seen anything like this before, but Mercer had. And it was around about then that she started to lose her humanity, because deep down she knew that there was no other way to *cope*.

That particular case had never left Mercer, and as a result it had haunted her. Not simply because of the gruesome nature of the case, nor because of the graphic crime scenes, nor even the fact that she felt no sympathy for the victims, mainly because they were utter scum. Admittedly, feeling no sympathy whatsoever for the victims did leave her questioning herself, though she quickly brushed that aside.

Instead, Mercer was haunted by two main things.

The first was that the case was never solved. Three murder victims at three different locations, none of the victims connected in any way other than the fact that they all had criminal records and had each inflicted misery on victims of their own. No murderer was traced, no connection could be found. They simply had to concede that a vigilante-like figure had butchered the victims, before dealing with the contrasting public responses. The media response was typically hysterical, with certain outlets going as far as to express deep sympathy for the victims. The general public opinion was more split; most people believed that karma had been dealt to the victims but some were vocal in their concerns of the nature of vigilantism and where the buck stopped on dishing out justice.

The second issue that plagued Mercer was something she had never shared with anybody else however, and she wasn't about to start doing so. Shortly after the furore of the case died down, a suspicion entered her mind that she may have cracked it, but it was a suspicion that left her cold and one in which she never acted upon.

The Chief Inspector.

That old timer who could be gruff, blunt and moody, but who was the finest mentor she had ever known. A fear crept up on her that left her wondering whether the work had broken him, especially given the fact that the three victims had proven to be a burden to him, burdens whose escape from justice had left him deeply frustrated. She had often kicked herself for wondering as such, but over time she had come to accept that she believed it to be true; the Chief Inspector had butchered the victims and ensured that nobody found the bodies. She never told anybody out of a combination of loyalty to him and a fear that she may be wrong and thus land him in trouble whilst destroying their relationship. She had also feared the truth, however, hence why she delayed accepting it for so long, also fearing that if the job had taken its toll on him in such a manner, then what would it do to her...

Five years had passed since his death. She visited him regularly after his retirement, which came shortly after the closing of that dreadful case. He had quietly mellowed by the end, and she had found solace in his quirky humour, especially given his jokes at his own surprise that he had lasted so long. He had displayed sadness however at the fact that she had never had a family of her own, though he showed understanding at her explanation, especially since it matched so closely to his own. In many ways, they were kindred spirits as opposed to just teacher & mentor. He had died relatively peacefully, but he took so much with him to the grave.

Mercer knew that.

And now, a case not so dissimilar had fallen in front of her again. This time, however, there was no gruesome bloodshed, no scenes of horror, no underlying theme to the victims like criminal records. There was simply a long list of dead bodies, all executed in quiet fashion, often through suffocation or choking as opposed to butchering and massacre. Minor connections had been established, such as a couple of victims here and there having worked together or gone to school together, but that's often where the links ended.

"Are you alright, ma'am?"

Mercer snapped her eyes up from the floor, her eyes wide as she looked at Jones.

The young man paused as she stared at him, before asking again "Are you alright? You seemed to leave me for a moment."

Mercer paused a little more, her eyes drifting around the room, before she answered "Yeah. Yeah, I'm fine, kid. Just lost in thought."

"You're one of the best, ma'am," Jones said honestly. "Don't let this one beat you up."

Mercer sighed, and was about to respond when the door swung open, and one of their colleagues, PC Williams, burst in, brandishing a letter. The same age as Jones, Williams faintly reminded Mercer of herself, albeit the younger woman was bubblier & more innocent than Mercer had been back in the day.

"Ma'am, this has come through!" the younger woman panted, handing the letter to her superior.

Mercer took it, and glanced her eyes over the front of envelope.

To Whomever is Leading the Case of the Countless Missing Bodies...

The envelope had already been opened.

"Safety precaution, ma'am," Williams said, almost reading the look on Mercer's face when she saw the torn open envelope.

"Don't worry about it," Mercer replied, glancing up at Williams before asking "Has anything else arrived with this?"

"Nothing, ma'am," Williams answered.

"Okay," the older woman responded quietly, returning her gaze to the envelope.

Williams paused for a moment, glancing at Jones with caution, who also appeared to be holding his breath.

"Is there anything else I can do for you, ma'am?" Williams asked, eventually.

"Not at all, doll," Mercer answered, again looking up at her colleague, albeit with a small smile this time. "Thank you."

Williams returned the smile, gave one to Jones as well, who also returned one, and then left the room.

"What the bleeding hell have we got here...?" Mercer asked out loud, as she took the letter out of the envelope, and began to read it.

To Whom This May Concern,

I've no doubt you must be frustrated at your inability to catch me, and for that you have my sympathy, though I've also no doubt you care not for that. I must also inform you that you will find no luck in solving this case, not truly anyway. I will inform you as to why at the end of this letter.

My life has been a simple one. I've been fortunate enough to get by quietly, go through School, College and University unlike my family before me, and do my best to afford myself a life that never asked for much but always gave me what I needed. I was most fortunate to be able to find the love of my life and begin a family. Some in life are tormented by their circumstances, others by happenstance completely out of their control. I have been lucky to never have to experience any true ills or pains or suffering as such, and I have always been aware of my fortune in that sense.

That was until my life came crashing down, and everything I held dear was lost.
Life was going by so peacefully, so quietly, and then one day... One day it was destroyed. You hear it happen every now and again, a tragedy of sorts that ends lives or leaves them in ruins. In my case, it was one of those avoidable motorway incidents. You know the type, somebody driving with reckless abandon and

innocents are taken. The innocents in question that day were my wife and children. The man responsible for their deaths survived with cuts, bruises and a broken leg. More importantly, instead of being dealt justice, the pathetic judge deemed a more fitting sentence to be rehabilitation for the man's alcoholism.

I wonder if you, someone within the force, has to regularly deal with that kind of injustice. I sincerely hope you are the kind of person who does your job because you believe in it, and if so, you must understand the anger I felt, and the fact that I had to find a way to cope.

You see, once my family was lost, life lost all meaning. Justice had to be served, and I cared not for the consequences. Humanity, for me, was a thing of the past. My family were dead, and my spirit was broken. He had to suffer; he didn't deserve to carry on living. And so, I found him. And I killed him. Although I was clever with that one, I simply made it look like he had drunk himself to death having snuck out of rehab. Kidnap and murder were probably what left me a shell of a shell, let alone a shell of the man I was, but I cared not. Justice was served.

Something then happened to me, something which has undoubtedly left you frustrated as body after body racked up. Though my life had been relatively pleasant, the loss of my family made me realise that there were a number of people who I had truly loathed at different stages of my life, and so I took the decision to remove them.
You already know how they died. You've probably already determined certain connections. I knew some of them in school, others in work. Others still are family, while some are family of

family. It matters not what their status is in relation to me, what matters is that they are dead.

You see, everything I cared for, that I loved, is gone. They're dead, and they're never coming back. And, you see, once you experience such trauma, and your humanity departs you, you realise there's nothing to hold you back from leaving this life with the kick in the balls it deserves. After all, if there's nothing left to love, and nothing left to lose, what's stopping you?

Anyway, by the time this letter reaches you, I shall be gone. I have committed evil deeds, and I no longer wish to continue this existence. I apologise to you and your colleagues for the significant inconvenience, but not for the deaths. They deserved what they got.

Don't bother looking for me, you'll never find my body.

I'll have made sure of that.

Silence reigned in the room.

Jones sat quietly, awaiting to see the letter himself, wondering what detail had left his superior so gripped. His thoughts drifted from darkened intrigue to concern when he noticed Mercer's hands beginning to vigorously shake, as she slammed the letter down on the table between them.

"Inspector Mercer," Jones began quietly, "what is it?"

For what felt like an eternity, Mercer sat in silence, staring into thin air, though she tried to control her tremor. A million thoughts spun through her mind, undefinable & almost impossible to comprehend. But the similarities she had been considering mere moments before the letter arrived were at the core of her thoughts, the cold rushing sensation thrashing through her as though a crude message had been sent to her through an even cruder, uneven form of Déjà vu.

And as she gazed into space, she almost thought she could see the Chief Inspector standing in the corner of the room, hands in pockets, his face sullen and tired yet sympathetic to her, as though he knew what she was experiencing, as though he had done everything he had as a means of preparing her, but also as though he had never wanted her to suffer like he did.

The visage was gone before she knew it, before she could call out to him, and thus risk looking mad in front of Jones. Speaking of which, the younger man's face only displayed further concern by the time Mercer turned to face him.

"Talk to me, ma'am," he said, his tone soft but his intent to display strength clear.

Mercer looked him square in the eyes for a moment, before glancing back at the letter. Not taking her eyes away from it, she simply replied "The case is closed."

She gazed at it for another few seconds, before rising from the chair and heading towards the door.

"Wait, ma'am!" Jones called, quickly rising to his own feet to catch her before she left.

Turning tiredly to face him, Mercer said "Kid, help the others with some of the admin bollocks on this case and then get yourself home. You've been amazing. Honestly, you have."

"But ma'am, are we just giving up?" Jones asked with an almost youth-like exasperation.

Mercer breathed a silent chuckle, before answering "There's nothing to give up on, kid. We never even had a chance with a case like this. This was a man with nothing left, and he's just a ghost now. Just like so many others I can think of."

Jones swallowed a hard gulp, before asking "Are you gonna be alright, Inspector?"

The older woman smiled weakly before replying "I've gotten by for well over twenty years, young Jones. And like a great man wanted me to, I'll do what I've always done. I'll head home, pour one out and slap some Miles Davis on, and then I'll come back to work and do it all over again tomorrow. That's what I do to cope, because when we do this job, we need to cope. If we can't cope, then how can we do right by people?"

"But how do we do right by the families of these victims, Inspector?" Jones fired back a little too quick for Mercer's comfort.

After a brief pause, she replied "We can't. And coming to terms with that fact is something that'll require you to cope. And once you learn to cope, you can do right by the majority, even if every now and again a case like this one slaps you in the face and brings you to your knees. It's these cases you'll learn from the most. They'll haunt you to the end of your days, kidder, but they'll make you one of the best, just as they made me one of the best, and just as they made my mentor *the* best."

Jones nodded, before asking "But at what cost?"

Mercer's smile weakened but remained, as she said "Like I said, they'll haunt you but they'll make you one of the best. See you tomorrow, Jones."

"See you tomorrow, ma'am."

And with that, she was gone.

The Group of Five

"This is too much like a low budget horror film for my liking."

Sam's words left his mouth with too much of a tremble for his liking. He wasn't exactly trying to sound steely, but he certainly didn't intend to display signs of fear, either.

"All the better," Rebecca replied with a laugh. "Let's find out if all these spooksville rumours actually have any substance to them."

"As long as I get to stay on the ground floor," Jess butted in quickly. "Apparently the stairwell in this place is huge and I don't do heights. I get vertigo!"

"Pft! Vertigo?!?" Mark spat in amusement. "You're the type who jumps on a two-step ladder and all of a sudden you're in bleeding space!"

"Oi!" Jess responded, although she had to raise her voice over the hysterics of the others. "Don't take the piss, it's horrible when it sets in!"

"Alright, alright..." Luke, the fifth member of the group, interjected, "Let's just carry on and we'll be there in no time. Then we can determine where we go based on Jess' wuthering heights syndrome."

"Oh, don't you start," Jess replied, though whether it was heard by the others amidst a new wave of laughter, she couldn't tell. Her mood was already soured.

The five of them were embarking on a long-planned trip to an abandoned house up on the hilltop just outside of town. The town in question where they resided was where they had all been born and had lived all their lives, but this old house that could be seen from miles around had always intrigued them, particularly the likes of Rebecca, who loved a good haunted tale.

Abandoned for decades, but why nobody knew, this house had been particularly visible to all of them when walking home from school, both primary & secondary, and again now when they returned home from college on the bus. Just sitting there on the hilltop, almost dusty in the distance, and yet it remained visible in all weather conditions, even in the fog. It baffled most who saw it in such condition; one could be struggling to see twenty yards down the road at 7am on a misty, foggy morning but the house somehow found a way to defy nature & logic and stand out & be visible to the human eye.

Something else that had struck this five-piece group since childhood was the attitude of each of their respective parents to the old house. Indeed, even the parents of others they knew shared such attitudes. Attitudes of trepidation, concern and even fear, albeit somewhat unspoken. Nobody really liked to talk about the house, instead the replies to any questions about it would always be along the lines of "Don't ask me about it" or "It's dodgy that old place" or "Just something about it that's never felt right to me."

Very few seemed to wish to share what they had heard about it, and as such, intrigue among those who knew nothing about it only grew, as did rumour and loose tales. Such rumours & tales thus formed stories, and those stories became legends. The main question that lingered then was whether such legends were born of truths, however great or small, or were simply built on layer upon layer of fabrication. And to this group of five, that was a question that needed answering.

To give them something to build upon prior to setting off for the old house, the youngsters had focused on one of the legends that appeared to pop up more often than the others. This one in particular often seemed to centre around the supposed butchering of a group of visitors to the old place during its days as a hostel some one hundred & fifty years prior.

Apparently, another group of five had arrived at the hostel during their travels, needing to stay the night for rest & recuperation. Of the five, four of them were found the following day, massacred. The fifth was never seen again, not in the local area nor anywhere else, despite search parties being sent for him. The hostel was being run by a strict, elderly woman at the time who unsurprisingly came under great suspicion as a result of the crime, but her usually stoic nature crumbled under investigation, and she was quickly placed under supervisory care. Utterly horrified at the fact that such a travesty had occurred seemingly without her knowing, despite her being in the house at the time, she quickly deteriorated and passed away six months later. Her rapid decline quickly gave people the impression that she was innocent and thus had been genuinely traumatised by both the event and the early suspicion placed upon her.

The old house remained empty for a further eighteen months until it was seized by local authorities who duly placed it up for sale. It proceeded to change hands on a regular basis, roughly every five to ten years or so, for just short of a century, until it was finally abandoned roughly fifty years prior to this modern young group's trip. The constant buying & selling of the property birthed a rumour that the property was haunted, a haunting either brought about by unknown events prior to the massacre or simply by the massacre itself, and that the countless folk who had lived on the premises had experienced events that left them with no choice but to leave. Such supposed experiences had never been detailed, but it hadn't gone unnoticed that everybody who lived in the property always left town once they sold up, and not one ever took the time to return. It left a shadow over the town and its people, as though the old house was giving the area a reputation it didn't deserve. That probably went some way to further enhancing the dark legacy the old house possessed, and only strengthening the frowns the locals gave it whenever their eyes passed over it from a distance. Generation after generation had heard the rumours, not only of the travesty (or at least, dark rumours & legends like it) but also of how those who had lived in the house had felt the need to run and never turn back. The old house was almost like the leper of the town, bringing shame and discontent to those who called it home.

"I heard you could still smell the blood on the floorboards a century after the butchering," Rebecca was telling Jess, clearly enjoying the latter's discomfort a little too much.

"That's absolutely disgusting," Jess replied. "Are you telling me they didn't even clean the place?"

"Oh, yeah!" Rebecca answered with wide-eyed eagerness. "But the smell just never went away! It just lingered. You know how when you walk through your front door, the first thing you can smell is the expensive fragrances your Mum buys to cover up the fact that she doesn't do housework? Like that, but if they'd been imported in from Transylvania!"

"Oh my god, why are we ev-," Jess began, until it dawned on her, "wait, what did you just say?"

"Nevermind," Luke again interjected before any aggro could begin, "it's just a couple of minutes away."

"Banter," Rebecca whispered to Sam. Though the devilish grin was still on her face, she noticed how the latter still appeared to be uncomfortable with the whole trip.

"Come on pet, what's troubling you?" she asked him, her tomboyish nature poking through his more introverted senses, as she slung an arm round his shoulders. "Me and you against the spooks, you should be up for this!"

"Come on, Bec, you know full well I never wanted to come here," he groaned, slinging his arm around her waist in response to her shoulder hug. "If you'd suggested a horror night with a pizza, I'd be more upbeat, but this just feels like we're screwing about with something that shouldn't be screwed about with."

"Listen," she began to reply as her eyes burned holes in him, "I've wanted to see this gaff for ages. Once we're out, we'll get shot of these three and get back to mine for the night. Deal?"

Sam turned his eyes back to his friend whose cheeky expression pulled a small chuckle out of him. Sighing to himself, he replied "Deal. You owe me one."

"Don't worry about it, I'll be buying the food later," Rebecca grinned as she gave him a passive aggressive peck on the cheek and looked ahead towards the old house, which was quickly coming further into view.

"Seriously though," Sam said cautiously, "does the place still stink of blood?"

"It did fifty years ago, apparently," Rebecca answered. "As for now, well, we're about to find out."

While those two held onto each other as they walked, Luke & Mark were engaged in their own conversation, while Jess constantly glanced around in concern.

"Does your Dad know you're coming?" Mark asked Luke.

"Yeah, he thinks I'm mad but we had a laugh about it," the latter answered. "Mum doesn't know, though. I think she'd have locked me in the garage if she had any idea."

"Ha! I can imagine," Mark replied. "I didn't bother telling mine, I just said I was going out for a bit."

"Is that wise?" Luke asked as he raised an eyebrow.

"Why'd you ask?"

"Well, personally I think we'll wander around this old dump, get bored and then go home, but if something stupid happens, shouldn't they have some idea where you are?"

"Nah," Mark said with a little shake of the head. "We'll be fine, no need to stress 'em out."

"Hmm," was all Luke could muster in response. He turned his head towards Jess, asking "What about you, Jess? Told anyone you're coming?"

"Hey?" Jess let out, a little startled by Luke calling over to her. "Oh, erm, yeah I let my brother know."

"What did he say?" Mark asked.

"He thinks I'm stupid," came Jess' response. "To be perfectly honest, I completely agree with him. Not that I told him that."

"Of course not," Mark chuckled, "god forbid you let him score some easy points."

"Exactly!" Jess laughed, able to alleviate some of her tension thanks to a bit of harmless fun on her friend's part.

As the minutes passed by until they finally reached the old house, the five friends were able to put each other at ease, ensuring they arrived in good spirits, hoping to fulfill this ambition of experiencing this place for themselves.

"Legendary status awaits..." Luke said in mock drama. Once they actually reached the old house, all five of them found themselves on a peculiar middle ground psychologically. Gazing towards it from the end of the large front garden, immediately there was a mutual vibe amongst them that seemed to silently scream "Is this it?" yet simultaneously the house seemed to give off even eerier vibes than previously thought possible.

How could it be that one could be so unimpressed yet so shook up at the same time?

"Last chance to turn back," Rebecca barked, her attempt at a confident, comedic rallying cry coming across more as an attempt at swallowing her own fears, not too dissimilar to Sam's earlier.

When no one replied, Sam was the one to speak up. "Let's just get this over with, shall we..."

In unison, the group began to step forward through the garden gates, walking down the stone walkway through the middle directly towards the large front door. Upon reaching the door, they noticed an old wooden sign had been nailed to it, and the sign carried an inscription: *lasciate ogne speranza, voi ch'intrate!*

"Isn't that Italian?" Mark asked the others absently, as he wrinkled his nose while staring at the sign.

"Yeah, I think so," Sam answered. "Can anybody read it?"

The others all shook their heads.

"Why Italian?" Luke questioned out loud. "Religious reasons, maybe?"

"Possibly," Sam replied. "Maybe a church goer did it. It looks as though it was nailed on decades ago."

Silence reigned briefly, as the group awkwardly gazed at the inscription, until Rebecca felt the need to get things going.

"Alright, come on, let's not waste any time."

She placed her hand on the door handle, and tried to open the door without success.

"It's bleeding locked!" she spat out. "Are you serious? We've come all this way and it's locked?"

"Maybe that's a sign we shouldn't be here," Jess mumbled, her eyes still fixed on the inscription.

"Bollocks!" Rebecca barked back. "We just need to get inside, is there any other way in?"

"Sod this," Sam muttered to himself before giving the door a good kick, and another, and another, as the door began to give away.

"Woah, woah, woah, what are you playing at?" Luke howled, his horrified expression matching that of Jess & Mark. "Are you mad?"

"Look, are we getting in there or not?" Sam replied with exasperation. "We've come up here, now let's just get inside and get on with it."

With that, he turned back towards the door and gave it one final kick. The door duly fell off its hinges and collapsed to the floor of the old hallway behind it.

After a brief pause, Rebecca turned to Sam and scoffed "Who knew you had such a kick."

Sam frowned in response, and gestured to the others to step inside. Rebecca was the first in without hesitation, but the other three took a moment to glance at each other.

"Are we doing the right thing, Sam?" Mark asked quietly.

"I've no idea," Sam answered solemnly, "but we've gone on about this place for too long to finally get here and then turn back. We'll be in and out before you know it."

Mark took a breath, sighed and nodded before stepping inside.

Luke turned to Jess. Her fear couldn't be hidden. When she saw Luke's determination, however, she too took a deep breath and nodded. Luke took her hand as a show of support, before leading her through the now doorless-doorway.

Sam took one last look back towards town, taking in the sights for a moment, before turning on his heel to join the others.

Once inside, he instantly felt a cold rush through him.

We've made a mistake.

The little voice in his head was right, but suddenly he felt like Jess during her shallow moments; he couldn't let anybody else score points off him over this.

"Oh my god, this place is freaky!" Rebecca's voice could be heard booming out from what appeared to be the living room. "Everything just feels dead!"

"Not exactly what I need to hear right now, to be honest," Luke muttered as he glanced back at Sam. "She's not exactly wrong though, is she."

"Not really," Sam answered with a weak half-smile. "It's easy to see why so many would say 'that place just feels wrong.' It feels like a wound in nature."

"Bleeding hell, Sam, that's deep even for you!" Mark chuckled as he headed towards the stairs. "I'm gonna be that nutter that goes up here first. No doubt some old bird will be waiting for me in a room marked 237..."

"I wouldn't even joke about that, at this rate," Luke said bluntly. Turning his face towards Jess, whose hand he was still holding, he asked "Do you wanna stay with me?"

"It's okay," she answered with a weak smile of her own. "I'll be a big girl, but I'll probably just stay in the living room while you wander around. I'll let Bec have a run around first."

"No need!" Rebecca answered as she suddenly appeared out of nowhere at the entrance to the living room. "It's all yours, Jess. Mark, you go one way up the stairs, I'll go the other, so we're exploring everywhere at once. You coming, Sam?"

Hoping to hide his nervousness, Sam answered "Nah, I think there's a library down here, so I'll have a glance in there. Might see if I can nick a couple of old classics while I'm here."

"You're gonna steal books from a dead house?" Mark asked incredulously. "Ballsy bastard! Fine. Luke, you coming up?"

"Yeah, I might as well," Luke answered as Jess made her way into the living room. "If I'm not watching Jess I might as well keep an eye on you two."

As those two lads headed upstairs, Rebecca hung back to stay with Sam for a moment.

"Hey, you sure you're not gonna join me?"

"Don't worry about me, go and have a laugh," Sam smiled at her. "Just keep your eyes open and be safe."

The two shared a quick hug, before Rebecca turned and made her way upstairs. Sam heard her call to Mark & Luke "You two stay on the first floor, I'm heading up to the second."

A quick chill ran through Sam. He had forgotten the second floor, which was the original reason for Jess wishing to stay grounded. Now he came to think about it, he had barely taken the time to properly examine the house when they arrived. Probably because he had seen it from a distance so many times that he didn't feel he needed to perform any additional close examinations, but now that he thought about it, the house looked even worse up close than they had presumed it would.

Maybe that's what had led them to immediately being somewhat dismissive of the property when they arrived, its decrepit state. Of course, why would it not be in such a state? It had been abandoned for so long, it's hardly like anybody was popping by every now and again for renovations. Maybe the last person to visit here was the one who had nailed the sign to the door. Speaking of that sign...

It lay on the floor near Sam's feet, and he glanced down at it briefly, the inscription feeling like a warning that everybody knew, but he couldn't quite put his finger on it. Wishing to shrug away any doubts and fears, he poked his head into the living room where Jess had sat down on a grand old chair.

"You alright, Jess?" Sam asked from the doorway.

"Yeah, I'm alright," she answered with an admirable attempt at a brave smile. "You have a wander around. I'll be here when you're all finished."

Sam gave a little nod in response, glancing his eyes around the living room, which he now realised was probably the biggest room in the house, taking up almost half of the ground floor area, before he turned back and headed in the opposite direction towards the smaller lounge area. A sunlit gleam poked through the windows as he wandered through, his feet treading over small shards of wood & glass as he walked. He was taken aback by how... empty this room appeared to be. The large living room Jess currently occupied at least had some of its old chairs for décor, but this room had been almost stripped bare. He looked towards an open doorway to the next room that he had noticed from a distance once they had entered the hallway earlier, and to his satisfaction his suspicions of a library were confirmed. Well, a small personal library anyway. It was almost a cul-de-sac of a room, with this doorway leading in from the small lounge being the only entrance and exit, with the walls hidden by row after row of shelves adorned with books, most of which must have been one hundred & fifty to two hundred years old. Sam's desire to pinch a few classics only grew as he cast his eyes over each aged spine, though Mark's words about 'stealing from a dead house' rung in his ears for a moment. Shrugging off any little doubts, he strolled around the room, occasionally running his fingertips over the books and appreciating the artistry of old hardbacks, even if he kept having to wipe dust from his fingers.

"I wonder what stories you lot you could tell," he said out loud, before silently chastising himself for realising the obvious; books contain stories, of course they have stories to tell! Of course, he was referring to the physical nature of the books as though they were carrying spirits of their own, and what stories those spirits could tell of the people who had read the books over time and the many people who had come through this old house. Chuckling to himself for both his brief silliness and the resulting self-chastisement, he continued to gaze admirably at the books around him, rather happy he had decided to come after all having landed upon this little treasure trove. He decided he was going to follow Jess' lead and kill some time while Bec & the lads were exploring, and so he looked a little closer with the intent of pulling out a book to read now before deciding which others he would take home with him. After his eyes skirted up & down & all around, they landed upon a blood-red leather behemoth that stood on the very bottom rung of one of the shelves. Peculiarly, while all the other books on the shelves were wedged up against one another, this one was stood in the corner on its own, at least a ruler's length away from any other book, as though it had been cast out by the other books like the unpopular kid in the corner of a classroom.

Or as if the other books feared its presence.

Sam paused for a moment upon hearing his inner voice whisper those words.

For what felt like a brief eternity, his eyes lingered on the book, until he almost drifted into autopilot and bent his knees to allow him to collect it. Straightening up, he turned the behemoth over in his hands. The blood-red leather was even more alluring in his grasp. The back and spine were devoid of any text, but the front contained a small, scruffy, silvery inscription just slightly over the middle.

Libro Malum

Sam didn't know what it meant, but he was more taken aback by how the inscription had been formed. It was as if somebody had dipped a blade in melted silver and scratched it into the leather. If the words themselves, whatever they meant, didn't leave a chill running up your spine, the manner in which they were presented certainly would.

Sam glanced up to look back through the doorway into the lounge. Nobody had followed him, and occasionally he could hear footsteps from above, so all seemed to be well with the others. Looking back down at the cover of the book, his intrigue seemed to fluctuate between increasing and waning. A part of him constantly told him to put the book back, that coming here was generally a bad idea that could get a lot worse should certain choices be made, while another part of him was telling him to just adopt a more laissez faire approach and not be so worried. He sat himself down to lean back against one of the shelves, irritated by his own conflictions. He paused again briefly to take a moment to take ahold of his thoughts, before finally taking a deep breath, biting the bullet and opening the book.

***

Jess cocked her leg across the other, letting out a sigh as she looked around at the terribly depressing place that she found herself in. The youngest of the group, having been the last to turn eighteen, Jess was somewhat of an enigma; often self-centered and egocentric, but undoubtedly in possession of a heart of gold. It was a heart of gold that she often failed to allow to truly flourish, however. Her friends, currently scattered around this disturbing old house, had quietly found themselves dismayed at how cold she had become, and yet found themselves equally baffled at how her seemingly true self, the good side of her, would pop out at seemingly random moments to remind them just why they were so fond of her.

The truth is, Jess herself knew she was becoming quite cold, and though she hadn't mentioned it, she had noticed her friends' collective discomfort at what she became when this negative side of her took control. She had noticed the varying glances, some of concern and others of disgust. In turn, she had silently told herself to change, but whether it was simply who she was becoming as she left her youth behind, she wasn't sure. Either way, she wasn't entirely comfortable with any of it. Just as she wasn't entirely comfortable with being here. Actually, scratch that, she wasn't comfortable at all being here. She had long joined in with the fun of wondering what this old place was like and what had truly gone on here in years gone by, but deep down she had never actually wanted to find out. Or, at least, she had never wanted to actually found out for herself first hand. She would happily have settled for somebody else doing the dirty work and for her to have found out the details via some second-hand news, but alas, she had succumbed to allowing her friends to drag her along. Maybe, in some egotistical way, she wondered if she would be able to bathe in some kind of plaudits if the others stumbled across anything. Maybe her name might end up in the paper with the others, or something like that...

There it is again, Jess...

That ego, that self-centeredness. Thinking only about how others can serve her needs & wants, and how she might be able to benefit. She often found herself like this, realising the crude decline of her morality, stumbling over herself in mental silence as she wondered why she was like this now, why the person she was becoming wasn't who she had wished to become.

She had no answers.

She glanced around again, and in doing so, wondered about those who had called it their home so long ago. She wondered whether such moral quandaries were suffered by those who lived through different times. Without wishing to blame the modern world for her ills, though she could hardly be blamed if she did to some degree, she wondered how the people of so long ago adapted to the natural challenges brought about by the handover of the self from youth to adulthood, and how these challenges were impacted by the world around them. She pondered on her insecurities, which she knew she wasn't alone in possessing, but at times felt alone in trying to understand and combat. She questioned her ambitions for what lay ahead in her future, whilst grimacing upon remembering just how much she feared the future.

How ironic, fearing the future whilst being seated in a place seemingly lost in the past.

Yes, fear of the future was something she suffered greatly with, but her pride and ego buried any such admittance of that fact when in the presence of others. People of eighteen are meant to gaze toward the horizon with hopes and dreams, hopes and dreams that they share with those around them. Jess would appear to be the exact sort of person who would be incredibly braggadocious when openly contemplating what the future held for them, but even when she did discuss it amongst her close-knit friends, she found herself struggling to deliver her lines with the energy & self-belief required to make others believe that she meant what she was saying. Truth be told, she had actually found herself wishing she could remain in the bubble she found herself in; alongside her friends, out of school but not quite into the big wide world, and with not an ounce of responsibility upon her shoulders. Instead, she was here in this house where she really didn't want to be, away from where she felt safe and comfortable. Although, being here almost reflected that she was away from the world that would soon ask so much of her, even if only for a moment, and so she almost found a sense of content and solitude perched here in this chair.

As she allowed a small smile to lift across her face, she wondered whether her friends were enjoying themselves. She could occasionally hear footsteps from the upper levels, and it almost gave her a sense of company, particularly as Sam was digging through the books, though she didn't begrudge him that, especially as she knew how much of a bookworm he was.

Not begrudging somebody. That wasn't so hard...

Then again, it *was* Sam, one of her best friends, so she could hardly pat herself too firmly on the back. The differences between herself and Sam, certainly these days, probably epitomized the somewhat bipolar nature of this gang of friends more than the disparity between any of the others, but despite the growing differences, there remained a stoic sense of loyalty between them. Momentarily, Jess thought she heard a sound emanating from where Sam had wandered off to, but it seemed to be nothing more than a crackle, and the sounds of the footsteps above quickly outweighed any minor noises from elsewhere.

Shrugging away any thoughts at what the noise could be, Jess leaned back into the chair as she folded her arms, trying to build up some of that friendship stoicism within her and rejuvenate some of her inner strength. Maybe coming here could work out for her, and not as a result of some petty newspaper appearance. Maybe travelling here, if only just to experience the place and then enjoy some much-needed solitude, if not to actually explore, was exactly what she had needed for some time. Being with her friends certainly helped, and seeing them enjoy themselves always put a smile on her face, even if she didn't always show it when she was in one of her dour moods. She realised, as she tightened her arms in a vice across her chest, that her friends were sticking by her despite who she was becoming, and that she owed them, as a show of appreciation for their loyalty and friendship, a considerable amount of effort on her part to change who she was becoming. She was only eighteen; she was hardly lost to nihilism and narcissism just yet.

She allowed herself a barely audible chuckle, the sound of which was followed by the same sound she had heard moments earlier. Her head quickly turned in that direction, and she held her gaze there for a few moments, but again, there was nothing. No movement, no further sounds, nothing.

A small frown grew across her forehead, with a little growl accompanying it from under her breath. It was all too easy to irritate Jess, as was often the case when Mark & Luke decided to play the roles of jokers. Perhaps that was why she could be ratty at times, because too often it was funny to watch her get on her high horse. She sighed at that little realisation, but she wouldn't hold it against the lads. All five members of the group had teased each other over the years, it was a key feature of their union, their ability to prod and poke each other whilst also being there for each other when they most needed their friendship.

Jess let her head drop as her eyes travelled over the floor. As they did, she remembered what Rebecca had told her about the blood and how its residue could still be smelt from within the floorboards. Thinking about it, Jess didn't know whether to be repulsed or intrigued, as she found herself fixated on those very floorboards below her.

Her nostrils pricked up as she tried to sniffle up any such smells that may have remained here for so long, but ultimately, she was never able to determine whether what Rebecca had told her was true. Just as she hadn't realised that the sound she had heard earlier had pricked up for a third time, resulting in somebody standing over her while she stared at the floorboards. Upon noticing that she wasn't alone, Jess swung her head upwards but the sound she tried to make never made it past her lips, as a sharp slash cut across her face with such force that it tipped her off the chair and left her face down on the ground.

Her consciousness quickly abandoned her, and within a matter of moments, so did her life.

Mark's displays of immaturity often hid a sense of leadership he felt he needed to possess in the company of his friends. Some may have mistaken this for misguided notions of needing to be the alpha male of the pack, but instead it was a genuine belief within him that he needed to look out for his friends. Sam was the reserved one, Rebecca was the eccentric, Jess was the modern stereotype, Luke was brash and he, Mark, was the wildcard. A wildcard that loved to play the fool, but did so with one eye always open. As such, he couldn't help feel a hint of irresponsibility in them being here, especially given both his own eagerness to be here combined then with the reluctance he had shown after Sam had kicked the door down. How could he have shown such weakness so late on when he had been one of those clamouring to come here for so long?

It was then that he realised the irony in him focusing on such matters when he was already on the first floor of this old house wandering around where many hadn't dared to tread in decades. In another room further down from him, he could hear Luke doing his own bit of exploring, while above him came the sounds of Bec's footsteps as she marched around with such eagerness. He had to chuckle at the latter; he wouldn't go as far as to call this Bec's paradise, but knowing her love for all things "spooksville" as she called it, he knew full well she'd be absolutely loving life at the moment.

Spooksville.

"Hmph," Mark let out, almost an amused humph that could be heard from somewhere between his mouth and his nose. Glancing around what he assumed was once a bedroom, he began to slowly stroll to allow himself a closer look at what lay before him. In all honesty, there wasn't much. As was the case downstairs, it seemed that various pieces of furniture had been taken when the old house was abandoned, with what remained seemingly damaged and thus deemed best left behind. That didn't explain that mini library downstairs, now Mark thought about it for a moment, but he quickly shrugged that off as something that simply couldn't be explained.

Dirt and shards of old furniture crumbled and cracked under his boots, as he found himself sniffing to see if he could determine if Bec was right about the blood within the floorboards. Alas, he simply found his senses being hit by damp of the slow-burning kind.

Peculiar.

The damp smell was certainly there, and it certainly seemed to hang in the air, and yet the house didn't seem particularly afflicted by it in terms of physical damage, such as patches in the corners of decaying walls and beams. Mark couldn't quite determine what he was trying to make sense of, but it was as though there was an affliction within the house that left it outside the realms of explanation and understanding. The house felt dead, and yet it felt as though a sense of life was preventing it from being truly dead. He didn't know whether to be quietly impressed by such a sensation, as he undoubtedly would've been had he learnt about it when talking about the old house while in the comfort of his own home, or bluntly disturbed. Given the reaction of his physical & psychological senses, it would appear to be a blend of both, as an electric rush of blood around his body was countered by an icy chill that momentarily left him frozen.

Gathering himself for a moment, Mark paused and took a second to listen out for the others, but he heard nothing unusual, and so gave his body a quick shake and looked to carry on. His eyes climbed the wall to his left, pausing once they reached an old, small picture frame. Amazingly enough, an old photo remained in its centre, and he stepped forward to examine it. This house had supposedly been abandoned for decades. This photo looked ever so slightly older, and in it stood a sole individual, a young man of say...

My age?

Indeed so, maybe a little older. Mark looked into the young man's eyes and saw fire, a vibrancy that exposed a desire to see the world. He was looking into the camera that threatened to seize a part of his soul, and instead faced it down with confidence and a grin that displayed just a hint of the kind of arrogance often seen in those who don't look down on others, but instead simply believe in themselves and their destiny. A young man with the world at his feet. But what was his story?

Mark found himself wanting to take the frame from the wall so he could examine it. Why, he wasn't really sure, but intrigue won over and he lifted it from its delicate hinges and carried it over to the window. There wasn't that much light poking through, but enough to allow him a clearer view of the picture. For the briefest moment, he thought he saw himself in the young man's eyes, but any silly hallucinatory blurs were quickly knocked away. He turned the frame over in his hands, and noticed a small piece of paper wedged into the back of the frame. Bemused, he gently dislodged it, finding a very old passage scribbled onto it. Allowing his surprise that the note was still eligible after so long to quickly subside, Mark quietly read it aloud.

"Our boy, who nipped out and never returned. May your adventures be legendary..."

Nipped out and never returned?

The icy chill that gripped him moments earlier returned with a ruthless whipping, leaving his heart feeling like it had been dropped to the depths of the oceans. Immediately, his words to Luke earlier on the way here rung in his ears.

I didn't bother telling mine, I just said I was going out for a bit... We'll be fine, no need to stress 'em out.

He hadn't told his parents where he was going. He had felt no need to, after all. He was prepared to take a minor dressing down later on once he got back and told them all about his wander around the legendary old house, especially knowing that once he had told them of what had happened, there'd be nothing more to discuss. That old intrigue would have been satisfied and no more would need to be said.

And yet, here Mark was, gazing down at the photo, into the eyes of a long-gone young man, eyes that continued to feel like his own, and he suddenly felt fear. Not like the weakness he felt he had shown earlier, weakness that had stung him so much when he prided himself on leadership. No, this was different. This time his concerns didn't centre around his need to present himself in a certain manner to his friends. Instead, he very much focused on the sheer audacity of them being here, in the face of all the rumours and legends, and in doing so he remembered all the different ways various people had coldly shrugged off any discussion of the old house, each of them bearing ill feeling towards it. There was something deeply wrong about this place.

As his thoughts continued to darken, the grip of fear lingering on his shoulders beginning to strengthen, Mark thought he heard footsteps on the stairs. Distracted for a split second, he wondered who of the two downstairs it could be.

Can't be Sam, he'll be too busy stockpiling books. So much for Jess staying down there, then. She must've gotten over the vertigo...

Allowing himself a chuckle at his friend's comedic misfortune, he tried to beat back the lingering darkness, and cast his eyes back to the photo. While he was eager to buckle himself up, he also liked the idea of some company, both for his own benefit and to ensure that he could keep an eye on his friends. Better off to start coming together again, making sure each other were safe before then setting off for home. Knowing Luke was the closest to him, and also wanting to get his take on the photo and the house as a whole, Mark casually called out to him over his shoulder, albeit while keeping an eye on the photo in his hands.

"Luke?"

After no response came, Mark tried again.

"Oi, Luke! Come in here, will ya!"

This time, a slightly muffled sound could be heard, which sounded vaguely like Luke telling Mark to come to him, instead.

Letting out an irritated growl, Mark turned on his heel with the intent of heading back onto the corridor and joining Luke in the other room.

He never had a chance.

As soon as Mark had turned around to face the door, he found himself on the receiving end of a daggered assault through his throat that went upwards through his jaw and ended upon the puncturing of the roof of his mouth. His mind howled and his eyes bulged in horror, as both the impact & nature of the sickening blow assaulted every ounce of his being. Most of all, however, the horror that shone in his eyes produced final tears before they fell lifeless, tears triggered not only by his death, but also by the final thing he saw.

Like Jess, Luke was somewhat of an enigma within the group. While he could display hints of arrogance at times, often as a result of his belief in his own capabilities which could in turn be expressed quite abruptly, he certainly had a straight head on him. This was seen most commonly whenever he felt the need to defuse potential bust-ups within the group. He was more than happy to engage in banter, himself, as had been the case many times, but he also knew when to step in to prevent the group becoming fractured over silly jokes.

Privately, he had seen this little expedition as something of a coming-of-age opportunity for the group. Though it was hardly something like climbing Kilimanjaro, the friends were daring to tread where few in the town had ever considered, and it was something they had spoken of for years. Finally doing so would represent the fulfilling of a collective dream, however silly that may sound, and once it was done, they could leave the house behind once and for all, both literally & metaphorically. For what it was worth, Luke was the probably the least intrigued by the whole thing out of the five of them. He certainly appreciated the allure and the legends, and he undoubtedly had questions of his own regarding the secrets this old house possessed, but that was about as far as it went for him. Instead, a small part of him was more drawn to the ego trip of the whole thing rather than getting answers from the house itself. The idea of being part of a group that went looking for the truth and came back to tell everybody about it was quite alluring. That notion had actually popped up once in conversation with the others, and Luke had noticed how Jess had been instantly drawn to the possibility, before shrinking back, almost in shame. Luke, in turn, had quietly found himself disagreeing with Jess' sudden moral crisis; why worry about coming across as greedy when there was the opportunity for reward? While life wasn't purely about reward, Luke certainly believed that one shouldn't be concerned about benefitting from one's efforts, especially when fully deserved. Luke had, admittedly, like the others, been taken aback by Jess' change of character over time, especially when her tendency to be quite self-centered had shown itself a little too often for his liking. However, he also believed that a little ego did nobody any harm, especially if it acted as a mechanism for pushing someone in the right direction. Though he wasn't keen on Jess' self-centeredness, he was keen on Jess in general, and so was eager to find the time to have a little chat with her just to get her on the right track. But there was plenty of time for that.

Egocentrism aside, he now found himself in a dingy little room just down the corridor from where Mark was rooting around. Rebecca's footsteps could be heard above, and no doubt she would be dictating the assessment of the old house on the walk home. Regardless of whether she would be enthusiastic or rather subdued, she would be nattering away at the front of the group, which would probably allow Luke to accompany Jess at the back. Both of them would be able to quietly express their happiness at seeing the back of this old mess without ever having to worry about coming back, and then they could discuss things going forward.

Luke allowed a little smile to creep across his face at the thought. Yes, he had always had a thing for Jess, and deep down he believed the feeling was mutual. As such, he had slowly expressed little shows of affection and support for her over time, as he had done when they arrived here, without ever going as far as to specifically ask her out. Again, there was plenty of time for that. Right now, however, in this aforementioned dingy little room, he found absolutely nothing of interest. The others, Bec in particular, would have no doubt found something to focus on in even the most minute sense, but nothing about this place, or even just this room, stood out to Luke. He didn't know whether to be irritated by that or just underwhelmed. Any underwhelming feeling would centre on a perceived sense of belief that the house ultimately was an overrated, decrepit old shell which deserved to be put out of its misery and knocked to the ground instead of creating stories and legends that would continue to fester in the minds of the town's folk. Any sense of irritance would stem from a rather ego-driven belief that any special features of the house would almost certainly be easy to spot for Luke, and so if no particularly special features existed, then it only tapped into the belief that there was nothing here to see nor experience.

Ultimately, though this was the coming-of-age expedition Luke hoped it would be, it would prove to be a rather disappointing endeavour. With nothing to distract him in the room, he returned to his own thoughts, where to be perfectly honest he felt more comfortable. He'd rather allow himself to drift off until the others pulled him out of his slumber than simply stare at each wall of this room hoping that a speck of dirt would tell a story.

And so, his thoughts again returned to Jess, though as they did, he heard a little thump from below him. He did a quick double-take for a moment, glancing back at the doorway leading back to the corridor, as though looking in that direction would tell him what the sound represented, but after staring at the doorway for a few seconds, he quickly shrugged it off and returned to his thoughts. No doubt it was probably just Sam dropping one of the many books he intended to take home.

Heh, nerd...

Not that Sam's nerdiness irritated Luke, quite the opposite in fact, they were good friends after all. Luke just preferred to express his intellect differently. Sam didn't actually like to express his intellect at all, now Luke came to think about it, instead preferring to remain in the background and out of the spotlight. With that being said, that could potentially kibosh any potential public attention the group could achieve if they did actually find something of note, here.

Damn!

Resting his jaw in his hand for a moment, Luke actually began to wonder of a future where the group could quietly disband. Of the other four, he would undoubtedly want to keep Jess in his life, and probably Mark as well, but as time went on, though he would always be fond of them, he couldn't particularly imagine remaining in touch with Sam & Bec. They were all changing, and while he would always be immensely grateful for their friendships, he began to believe that they would only be keeping in touch with each other for purely sentimental reasons as opposed to actually having anything in common. It may appear cruel and callous, but it was something he would probably need to closely consider in the coming months, especially with their time at college coming to a close. Though he was eager not to bring forward the future in such a hurry, he also didn't intend to sit by as the future fell out of his control. With that being said, he quietly told himself that by the end of the year, Sam & Bec would definitely be doing their own thing, Mark may or may not be in the same boat, and that he would have finally grown a pair of nuts and made things official with Jess.

Sounds like a plan...

Another little grin, or maybe more of a smirk, grew across his face as his fingers stroked his jawline in appreciation of his own sense of brilliance.

Maybe being an egomaniac isn't such a bad thing. Maybe this house did have something to offer me after all...

Indeed, maybe that would be the legacy of this house, a little spirit within telling him to indulge in his own self and not bother worrying about morality. A little lesson learnt for him to take away.

As his smirk was accompanied by a small chuckle, he faintly heard footsteps coming up the stairs.

Ah, she decided to ascend after all...

Now he thought about it, why bother waiting until they were on the way home? He could use this quiet little space to have a chat now! They could be a couple before they even step back outside!

"Is that you, Jess?" he called out, an audible hint of amusement in his voice. "Decided to come here and join me, instead?"

He slapped his hands on his hips as a sly smile spread out and replaced his grin. As his thoughts spun around as to how he could phrase what he needed to tell her, those same thoughts briefly overwhelmed his senses, cushioning any audible sounds coming from down the corridor. After a minute or so passed without Jess appearing to make her presence felt, Luke managed to get a grip of himself and swung around full of intent. Balls to a plan, he was going to go all guns blazing, take Jess to one side and tell her how he felt. He could feel energy burning around his eyes, eyes he was eager to lock with Jess' as he finally said what needed to be said. Now he thought about it, all he wanted to do was see her. He was starting to feel somewhat sentimental all of a sudden, almost feeling as though the only purpose his eyes had at that moment in time were to look upon the girl he had long known as a friend, but who he now wanted to be so much more. For the briefest moment, he thought he saw her as soon as he turned around.

Instead, for an even briefer moment, he saw someone else. That was, until one of his eyes, his left to be precise, fell victim to a daggered strike that punctured so deep it completely ruptured Luke's senses. The dagger was held for a moment, before being brutally ripped back out. Luke's body shook, then dropped to the old wooden floor beneath him.

Dead.

Rebecca had reached the top floor of the house like a kid rushing down the stairs to get to their presents on Christmas Day. The fact that she had needed to go upstairs in contrast to the descent seen on December 25th every year hadn't passed her notice. Whereas Christmas Day was full of joy and light, this house and its history were full of decay and darkness. Not that she was an entirely cold soul, she merely just found fun in all things spooksville and horror. She was actually incredibly bubbly, at least when she was in the company of people that she felt comfortable with. Otherwise, she preferred to stay in the background of society. That was probably a key reason for her love of philosophical darkness; where the majority of society recoiled from what they didn't know, Rebecca was eager to look into the abyss. And if the abyss were to look back into her, then she'd happily say hello, have a laugh, pull her head back into the light and carry on with her day. She could be cynical & sartorial, but at her core, she simply wanted to be able to laugh and get on with her day.

As for this old house, Rebecca had first heard the stories from her slightly older brother some twelve years earlier. In addition to her view of society, her brother had also influenced her love of horror and the darkness, but he had done so in a delicate and fun way as opposed to the stereotype of the cruel elder sibling who would tease and taunt the younger brother or sister for kicks. He had utilised comedy as a means of ensuring that when his little sister would inevitably come across an uber scary horror flick when she was older, that she would be prepared for it and thus would be able to avoid the sheer trauma often experienced by mere casuals. His theory had proven to be successful, and as such it took a great deal to give even the mere shivers to Rebecca.

"You see, Bec," he had once said, "media is a reflection of society, and so these movie companies make horror films to both scare people and bring out the worst in people. If you're prepared for the scares and can even see the funny side, then you're nullifying their agenda. And then, when you actually come across something genuinely creepy, you're not only prepared to encounter it, but you can appreciate it for its legitimacy as opposed to being in awe at other fallacies."

He had said this to her a couple of years earlier, when she was sixteen and he, eighteen. By then, her intellect had long begun to shone through, and so he felt comfortable going from merely helping to prepare her for life's ills to actually testing her capacity for seeing through the fog of lies created by society and its puppet masters. Though she had long been close to her four friends, those who had travelled with her to the house, particularly Sam, her relationship with her brother was one she had cherished. Indeed, her dream had long been to come here with him, either in addition to her friends or instead of them in the event of them chickening out.

As it was, her friends hadn't chickened out, despite any concerns they may have possessed.

Nor were it possible for her brother to even have the opportunity to be here with her.

Just six months after he had uttered those words to her, about media being a reflection of society, she bore witness to another reflection of the world in which she lived in. Rebecca and her brother would often take it in turns nipping out to the shop to get snacks and essentials for the house when their parents didn't need to do a "big shop," and one simple Friday night it was supposed to be her turn. However, on her way home from college, she had gone over her ankle getting off the bus, and within an hour or so the aforementioned ankle had swollen up so badly that walking was simply out of the question. As such, her brother had humorously huffed and puffed before declaring that it mattered not, for he would take up the mantle and make sure he got something to soothe his sister's pain. It was usually a simple five-minute walk there, a couple of minutes gathering bits and paying for them, before another five-minute walk back.

But not on this day.

It wasn't uncommon for a couple of extra minutes to be added on if either the brother or sister had casually bumped into somebody they knew or were even chatting to the shopkeeper, but when half an hour had passed since her brother had left the house, Rebecca and her parents knew something was amiss. Her Father took it upon himself to head out and see, just to make sure everything was okay, but instead came rushing back within minutes utterly mortified. Rebecca's brother had never made it inside the shop; instead, he had been brutally assaulted for no reason other than cruel kicks by some miscreants lingering outside. The scum quickly dispersed, but the shopkeeper just as quickly rang for an ambulance. Once Bec's Father had reached the shop, the shopkeeper told him everything, leading the Father to rush back to the house in panic with the aim of collecting his wife and getting to the hospital as soon as possible. They never saw their son alive again. He hadn't simply been assaulted, he had been stabbed in the heart, and was tragically dead-on-arrival.

Rebecca, having been left behind due to her ankle, had been left to stew over her fears for hours, until her parents finally returned and relayed the horrific events that had made that evening the worst in her young life.

She had quickly descended into a bludgeoning depression, one that had threatened to obliterate her time at college. Thankfully, she had her four friends and they had been there for her, though there was only one of those four who had seemed to truly understand her pain, even though he had never experienced anything of that magnitude, himself.

Sam.

Sam just seemed to be there in a way that went beyond anything she could ask for. The two of them had always been closer to each other than they had the others, but even then, she had found herself amazed by the level of empathy he had displayed for her, and their friendship had only strengthened as a result. He had had his own long-term personal issues, most often centered around his anxiety and lack of self-worth, as well as a sense of not having a proper place in society, the latter of which Bec could familiarise with extremely well.

Over time, Bec began to realise just how much Sam came out of his shell when he was around her. Not around her when the others were there, but specifically when the two were just in each other's company. She had no doubt that the increasingly more outgoing personas and tastes of Jess, Mark & Luke were contributing factors to this, particularly as Bec & Sam's own tastes and personas, much more reserved &

philosophical, were beginning to contrast so heavily with the other three. Regardless, Rebecca & Sam's friendship was quietly blossoming in ways neither could have anticipated, so much so in fact that the two of them had, for some time, secretly been planning to slowly slip away from the others as time passed. The intention was not to abruptly just cut themselves off, but instead allow nature to run its course and spend less & less time with the others to the point where their absence would simply no longer be seen as out of the ordinary. College had, unsurprisingly, changed all five of them, but there was no doubt that this group of friends were on the verge of splitting into two. Thankfully, there was no malice involved, it was simply a matter of old friendships running their course, impacted by the age-old phenomena of people changing as they matured.

Additionally, another factor had contributed to Bec & Sam's changing view of their friends. The two of them had privately shared a kiss some months earlier, and while they weren't entirely ready to view themselves as a couple just yet, they both knew that they were heading in that direction. Once it was official, they knew it would go hand-in-hand with their split from the others, a kind of "coming-of-age" in which the two of them would go their own way while the others would embark on their own new journeys.

As Rebecca stood in the doorway of the first room to her right upon reaching the second floor, she found herself frozen momentarily. Her focus for a moment had purely been on Sam, and everything she was experiencing as the two of them grew closer. Though a small smile grew across her face as she thought of him, she also reminded herself just how important it was that she was here. Yes, of course, she was giddy about the spooksville factor, but as she looked around, she couldn't help but imagine what her brother's face would be like as he too gazed around at this old place, the two of them having finally journeyed here to discover the truth.

In all honesty, she couldn't help but feel like he would be shrugging his shoulders at this particular room. It was dingy, like most of the house, and on top of that, it was empty.

Meh...

She hadn't actually told the others that her desire to come here had been inspired so heavily by her brother's memory. Even Sam wasn't entirely aware, though he knew that Bec & her brother had intended to come here, something the others didn't know. Bec had refrained from emphasizing to Sam that her desire to see this place for her brother was such a key factor out of wishing to avoid any kind of emotional blackmail. She knew Sam wouldn't see it that way, but she still didn't want to put him in that position where he felt like he was coming because of such emotional pressure. As for the others, well, given that Bec & Sam would soon be leaving them behind, she felt no need to divulge such personal detail. She remained fond of Jess, Mark & Luke, and would always be thankful for their friendships that went back well over a decade, but she was quietly looking forward to them having a significantly reduced role in her life.

Not wishing to focus on that too much, however, she stepped back out onto the corridor and headed towards the other rooms. There were only two, and the first was identical to the one she had just left; empty, dingy and a disappointment. Bec made a point of casting her eyes to all corners of the room to make sure she wasn't missing anything, but quite frankly, there wasn't anything to miss.

She let out a little grunt, quickly left this second room and headed for the third.

Same again.

Dingy. Empty. Disappointing.

Her face wore a humorous look of frustration, and she found herself seriously hoping that the others had found something worthwhile to make all of this at least somewhat memorable.

A little noise could be heard below her, and she paused for a moment, leaning back out of the doorway to look back down the corridor towards the stairs. Hearing nothing more, she shrugged her shoulders and moved further into the third room. Again, she saw absolutely nothing of any note or spectacle, and as she reached a far corner, she turned and slumped down the wall so she could sit and just ponder while the others did whatever they were doing.

"You wouldn't have missed much, big brother," she muttered aloud. Now she thought about it, given that he was a constant source of advice, she remembered what he had once said about constantly keeping one's eyes open so not to miss the life lessons provided by even the smallest occurrences. Coming here provided a number of those, she imagined, particularly when considering the need to remain grounded, to not allow oneself to be easily consumed by excitement, and to never allow disappointment to nullify one's soul. Rebecca chuckled at the latter, especially given both the disappointment of this old house combined with the fire that had burned within her brother's soul, a part of which she genuinely believed she now carried with her at all times.

Further noise could be heard below, which Bec suspected was likely to be Jess joining Mark & Luke. Alternatively, she thought, maybe Sam had found something of note in the books and wanted to share it, though if that was the case then Sam was more likely to join her here than tell the others.

Deciding that she just wanted a few moments' peace until the others came for her, she closed her eyes and just allowed herself to rest. The noise below continued, seemingly little bumps or what not, but again Bec just assumed it was the others messing around. There was undoubtedly movement coming up the stairs, so that must have been Jess, and maybe the lads were running around having a laugh.

A few more moments passed and more footsteps could be heard, as though someone was now coming to the top floor.

"Sam?" Bec called out instinctively, her eyes popping open as she did.

No answer came.

"Who's there? Has something happened?"

Again, no reply.

Less than impressed at the idea of the others playing some kind of game, Bec rose herself up and headed for the corridor, turning left immediately upon exiting the room and heading for the top of the stairs. But there was no one there.

Nobody waiting at the other end of the corridor, as it seemed there would be based on the footsteps. Flummoxed, Rebecca leaned onto the balustrade and peered down to the bottom of the stairs. Quite unnervingly, there was space in between the stairwell for a straight drop from this angle, right down to the ground floor.

"Oi," she called out, "what's everybody doing?"

For the third time, nobody answered.

Until, from behind, a voice unlike any she'd ever heard before spoke with a tongue that sounded like something she'd never wanted to hear in her life, and as it spoke, she completely froze in fear.

"Raggiungi la cima, colpisci il fondo."

For a moment, she couldn't tell if the voice was emanating from behind as it seemed, or was actually booming around her mind. Either way, she didn't have long to think.

A violent force thundered into her back and all she knew was that she was falling right down that gap in the stairwell, experiencing that straight drop to the ground floor.

She hit the bottom with the most sickening thud. She quickly found herself caught in a middle-ground between total numbness and sheer agony, the former reflecting her life ebbing away and the latter representing the causation.

Before she died, her killer descended from above to join her. Barely enough life remained in her eyes to allow her to see, but what life did remain gave her the chance to identify the one who had sealed her fate. Once she had done so, her final moments were consumed by a torturous guilt, and with all her might, she used her dying breath to whisper "I'm so sorry..."

"What the bleeding hell *is* this?"

The words seemed to escape Sam's voice without his permission, drifting out in a barely audible tone. The book appeared to be full of hand-written text, predominantly in Italian if he had to guess, with the occasional English translation. What he couldn't understand was why the existing text up to a certain point appeared to have been spoiled. It was almost as if someone didn't want the reader to know what the book was trying to tell them. He flicked back to the early pages to have a quick glance at the contents list, and found a similar pattern. All the listed titles for each section of the book had been spoiled, as though they had been ticked off like items on a shopping list. All but one, however, that being the last section of the book.

It was titled *The Group of Five*.

A shiver ran itself up Sam's spine; it was as though his eyes had been trying to find this particular title, searching for what he had been looking for. Or maybe, what he had been meant to find. Wishing to try and combat any unnerving sensory attack on his physical form, he straightened his back firmly against the book shelf he was sat leaning against, hoping aimlessly to strengthen himself against any further nervous moments. Once he was semi-satisfied with the added tightness in his back, he paused for a moment, and simply stared at the unspoiled title near the bottom of the contents list. It had been scrawled in an almost haphazard manner, as though scratched into the paper by the ink-dabbed claws of a demon. Wishing to wait no longer to discover whatever this book had to reveal to him, he hurriedly turned over the countless pages until he landed on the section in question.

Immediately, he found himself succumbing to further bafflement. This section was seemingly a tale depicting the aforementioned "Group of Five," and instantly the depictions matched those of Sam and his friends. Their physical features, their characteristics, their histories, both individually and as a unit. The tiniest of voices in his mind begged him to toss the book aside instantly, but his intrigue quickly brushed away any such suggestions. He read of the three young men and the two young women, a collective of modesty, intelligence & loyalty blended with ego, ignorance & betrayal. These descriptions seemed to catch Sam off guard somewhat, until he read of how the group began a journey that had long awaited them.

Long awaited them.

As though not only had Sam & his friends long desired to come here, but as though the house itself had awaited their arrival.

"Behave," he muttered aloud to himself.

Continuing on, the storyteller, whoever it was, appeared to mock the group for both their ignorance & supposed "great error" upon arrival, but declared that all had fallen into place as each member found their destination within the house. Whereas the previous details about the group were minute while still appearing to match Sam & his friends to a tee, now the story took things up a notch, with each member being given a specific title. The five were declared to be 'the modest man,' 'the enthusiast,' 'shallow gold,' 'the joker' and 'the betrayer.' Once more, the choice of words left Sam reeling, particularly as his fears grew that the story was their own. If that wasn't enough, what came next was undeniably haunting.

The modest man quickly found solace in knowledge and revelation, while his secret lover, the enthusiast, rapidly ascended to her destination at the highest height.

Secret lover?

Again, the small voices in his mind returned, begging him to walk away while the choice remained his own. For a moment, he listened to them, but he quickly found himself pulled back to the book, as though it was engaged in battle with those small voices for Sam's focus.

The enthusiast was soon lost in her own thoughts, placing particular focus on why she was here and what the future held for her. Elsewhere, however, the shallow gold was engaged in a conflict of her own, tussling with her self-centered nature, whilst trying to tap into the obvious good in her heart as a means of becoming a better woman, for the benefit of not only herself but also her friends. The joker, meanwhile, was reflecting on his responsibilities to his friends while learning of a story similar to his own.

A story similar to his own?

Lastly, the betrayer's true form was beginning to show, as was his arrogance, as his plots for the future began to unfold in his mind.

Sam was on the verge of heeding the advice of the small voices, ready to toss the book aside, call out to the others and leave, never to return to this godforsaken place. A mistake had indeed been made in coming here, but if there was even the slightest chance it could be rectified, Sam wanted to take it! That was, until more of the text caught his eye.

All but one of these young fools have made their final journey, and indeed their final destinations are about to be reached. In the midst of their meaningless thoughts & feelings, the chosen one shall fulfill the deed and bring this story, the final one of the many that have come before it, to a close.

"The chosen one?" Sam muttered.

Turn away!

The voices in his head called out in desperation, but the book's victory was close to completion. Sam couldn't be pulled away from it now.

The deed shall begin with the fall of the shallow one. As she struggles to choose between right & wrong, she will need worry no longer, as her beautiful face shall be destroyed in one swift stroke, and the gold shall seep from her wound.

"Jess," Sam whispered. "Jess falls..."

Secondly, the self-appointed leader, the one known as the joker, will laugh no more, as his throat will be opened and the tongue that knows no limits will be brought to a most satisfying halt!

"Mark..."

Thirdly, the betrayer, plotting away his little plans, will never have the luxury of fulfilling such grandiose ideas as his ignorance shall be captured by the loss of a single eye, to reflect his most short-sighted nature!

"Luke..."

Finally, almost sadly, the enthusiast, the one who carries the scars of a broken heart. She who arrived here with such will and eagerness, must be sacrificed by the one who she loves the most. Where the others will meet their end with such cruelty, she must simply fall, thus representing the chosen one's descent into darkness...

Sam tried to scream, tried to howl "No!" but his throat was caught by a force he couldn't understand, and his eyes were almost forced to continue reading.

The Chosen One will fulfill the deeds! The one who will arrive here with hesitancy shall kick down the doors of evil and thus fall victim to its power! He is the final one of those chosen before him to fulfill the wishes of the great forces before he begins a journey anew to find the throne of the Lord of Darkness and stand by his side!

Sam began to seize up, shaking vigorously as the book fell from his grasp and crumpled on the floor beside his legs. He tried to fight whatever was happening to him, but it was a fight he was never, ever going to win. Almost as soon as the shaking began, it stopped, and Sam sat limp momentarily, until a most inhuman voice called to him from inside his head. As it did, it split his mind, causing brief but immeasurable pain, pain that only ended upon the words being called to him.

Fai quello che deve essere fatto!

The pain was gone. All feeling that he knew before was gone, replaced by an almost fire-fueled numb energy that ran through his veins. His head fell backwards and leaned against the book shelf for a few seconds, before his eyes fell back to the book. Moments earlier, he had no idea what could be found in the final pages, but he knew now. Aggressively gripping the book and pulling it back to him, he turned straight to the final page, where a crude, ancient-looking dagger was locked into the inside of the back of the book. He ran his fingers over the small, intricate locks which, as though needing the touch of evil in order to acquiesce, did so, allowing the dagger to fall into his lap. He held it both in his hands and in his gaze for just a moment, before rising to his feet and leaving the small library behind.

He strolled slowly through the lounge area he had wandered through earlier to reach the library, the same wood & glass shards crackling beneath his feet. His steps were taken almost methodically. There was no rush after all. Destiny can take a lifetime to achieve, a few extra minutes were hardly a cause for concern. He passed through the lounge and into the hallway, where the door he had destroyed lay beneath, almost dead, its purpose achieved, to lead the chosen one to his destination. Again, a crackling could be heard beneath his feet as he strolled through the hallway heading for the living room, where the shallow gold awaited him, the one they called 'Jess.'

He soon found himself stood at the doorway to the living room, and gazed upon her. She seemed vaguely irritated by something, but quickly allowed it to pass. She stared at the floorboards, and she began to sniff up as though trying to discover something, like an animal hunting for a scent.

Oh, the irony. Sniffling away like a predator on the prowl when she is destined to become the prey. The modest man stepped forward once more, again shards crackled beneath him. The shallow one had no idea he was there, with his dagger firmly in his grasp, ready to strike. Suddenly, she appeared to realise she wasn't alone, and he raised his arm as she turned her head. He didn't allow her the opportunity to respond to his presence; instead, he brutally slashed her across the face, robbing her features of their beauty, as the violent force tipped her off the chair and face down onto the floor. The modest man gazed down at his work, as the streams of gold flooded from her face and into the floorboards beneath her, where they would remain always.

The sounds of footsteps above caught his attention, and he whipped his head around with his eyes upwards, looking in the direction of the noise. Not taking those eyes away from what was above him, he stepped out of the living room, leaving the young woman's body behind as though it didn't exist. Once back into the hallway, he turned towards the stairs and slowly began to ascend, eventually reaching the first floor. The stairs resumed to his left for those wishing to reach the second floor, but ahead of him lay a brief corridor with a room immediately further forward on the left-hand side and then another room a little further on the right-hand side. Choosing the left-hand room first, the modest man approached it and as was the case downstairs, stood at the doorway watching his target. It was the joker, seemingly fixated with a picture of sorts.

Of course, the story similar to his own.

"Luke?" the joker called out.

Fool, the betrayer is too self-indulged to listen to you.

"Oi, Luke! Come in here, will ya!"

A voice came from the other room, the arrogant tones of the betrayer obvious even when muffled by these old walls.

The modest man's grip on the dagger tightened again in preparation. The joker growled to himself, and turned on his heel, seemingly intending to join the betrayer. Instead, he came face to face with the modest man who, with such ruthless efficiency, swung the dagger upwards through the joker's throat & jaw, before it came to a blunted halt when it punctured the roof of his mouth.

The joker's eyes bulged as his mouth filled with blood while his mind was awash with horrified confusion. He appeared to be torn between what horrified him more; the impact of his assault or the one responsible for it. Tears fell from his eyes, eyes that quickly fell lifeless, along with the rest of his body, which slumped to the floor as the dagger was abruptly ripped away from him.

The modest man cast one last look down at 'Mark's' body, before mockingly turning on his heel as the joker had done, moving back into the corridor and heading for the other room.

There, with his back to the doorway, stood the betrayer, the one known as 'Luke.' His ego burned out of him, with his hands triumphantly placed on his hips as he seemed to bathe in his own 'greatness.' So misguided, so short-sighted.

The betrayer appeared to brace himself, before swinging round to face the modest man. The swine must have been expecting someone else.

Regardless, he soon fell victim to a daggered strike that instantly obliterated his left eye and ran so deep that it completely destroyed his senses. The modest man held the dagger in place for a moment, enjoying the final of the cruel killings, before violently ripping it back out of the socket. The betrayer's body shook and dropped to the old wooden floor beneath him. Dead.

The modest man tucked the dagger away into his pocket.

That left just one more. The tragedy.

She, the enthusiast, was higher up on the second floor.

The modest man returned to the corridor and made his way for the stairs, ascending them once again. Once he reached the top, he paused, considering the necessary movements for this deed to be fulfilled as required. Gazing down the corridor, he turned his glance to his right, where an empty room would allow him to remain hidden until the enthusiast presented him with the opportunity to fulfil the deed.

The sacrifice.

"Sam?" the enthusiast called out from a room further down. The modest man gave no answer, instead just passing into the room and tucking himself just to the left behind the wall.

"Who's there? Has something happened?"

Her voice gave the modest man a peculiar feeling. The fire-fueled numbness in his veins was eradicating the one known as 'Sam,' but his history would always remain, as would his love for this young woman. Which is why her death would be a sacrifice as opposed to a cruel butchering like the ones experienced by the others.

The enthusiast's footsteps could be heard as she left the other room and made her way towards the top of the stairs, where she seemingly assumed someone would be there, waiting. Instead, there was no one, and her confusion was obvious. The modest man peeked around the doorway to watch her, with the dying embers of 'Sam' evident within him as his heart fluttered upon seeing her.

Not simply looking down the stairs, she also appeared to have noticed the gap down the middle, perfectly spaced for somebody to drop right through.

"Oi," she called out, "what's everybody doing?"

The modest man's footsteps, methodical as before, now walked almost silently as he left his hiding spot in the room and took his place behind her. He leaned forward ever so slightly, and spoke with a tongue so unlike the one he had possessed all the while he had been 'Sam,' and it froze the young woman in fear.

"Raggiungi la cima, colpisci il fondo."

So inhuman was the voice that left his lips, that the enthusiast was seemingly confused as to where the voice had come from; behind her or from within her.

It didn't matter.

The modest man leaned back this time, and with all the force he could muster, he pushed her over the balustrade. He didn't watch her fall, but he certainly heard her hit the bottom. He paused for a moment, as a thunderous sensation rippled through him, rocking him internally in the process. He let its brief energies pass, and began to descend down the stairs, all the way to the bottom, where the enthusiast lay dying.

The modest man watched her, as the life in her eyes left her more and more with every passing second.

Something became quickly obvious to the modest man, however, as he looked into those eyes. She knew who had condemned her to die in this old house, and she knew why. It was her who had brought him here, leading him straight to the fulfilling of the chosen one's destiny. Had she never brought him here, maybe their future together could have been bright. 'Sam' was slowly dying, too, inside of the modest man, but this woman, the enthusiast, would be with him always on the journey. The poor woman locked eyes with the modest man and, with such sadness, whispered "I'm so sorry..."

His gaze was cold, but her words allowed 'Sam' to pass peacefully within him. He watched her until she finally died, before heading towards the front door and into the open world. He glanced back one final time, before heading off for good.

He was gone.

Printed in Great Britain
by Amazon